Christmas

At Mimosa Lake:

Angels on High

Dearest Aunt:
A little light
reading for
the holiday —
But then —
Angels are always good
reading —
Thank you for having my
at Christmas
Love,
Niece

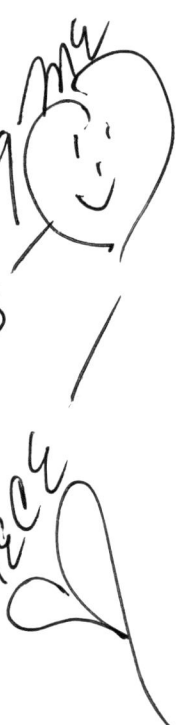

K.S. Wuertz

KSWuertz Publications
2015

Always to God:

"…For he will command his angels concerning you to guard you in all your ways; They will lift you up in their hands, so that you will not strike your foot against a stone.'"
Psalm 91: 11-12 NIV

Written with Thanksgiving to God
for His Son,
Jesus Christ

And to the many angels – in all their forms
I've had the honor of knowing
God has blessed me, He has blessed me indeed!

Merry Christmas from Mimosa Lake
To One and All

MIMOSA LAKE NEIGHBORS

Mimosa Lake Road

Smythe, Elmont & Victoria
Ravioli

Jehan, Joos & Mallie
(Emmanuel)

Fern Drive

Clintston, Harris & Peroze, Lucinda
Sammi

Potts, Herbert

Roach, Zigler & Juliet
Roman

Sheldon, Franklin & Beverlee
(Ellenour, Nate)

Cole, Tim & Teresa
Wolfman

Ivery, River & Thadius Sandberg
*Levi, Tobias, Vincent, Poppy,
Sugar, Angel*

Forest Drive

Crayton, Dock & Trixie)
Duke, Princess

Daniels, Jack & Nakita
Baby Grace, (Malkirk)

Owens, Alvin & Peggy
Bridget, Taffy, Harry

Wright, Missy
Amelia, W, Bunny, Jet

Lemonn, Georgia
(Felicia,), Mr. Mittens

Rolfes, Todd
Medea, Princess, Nevo

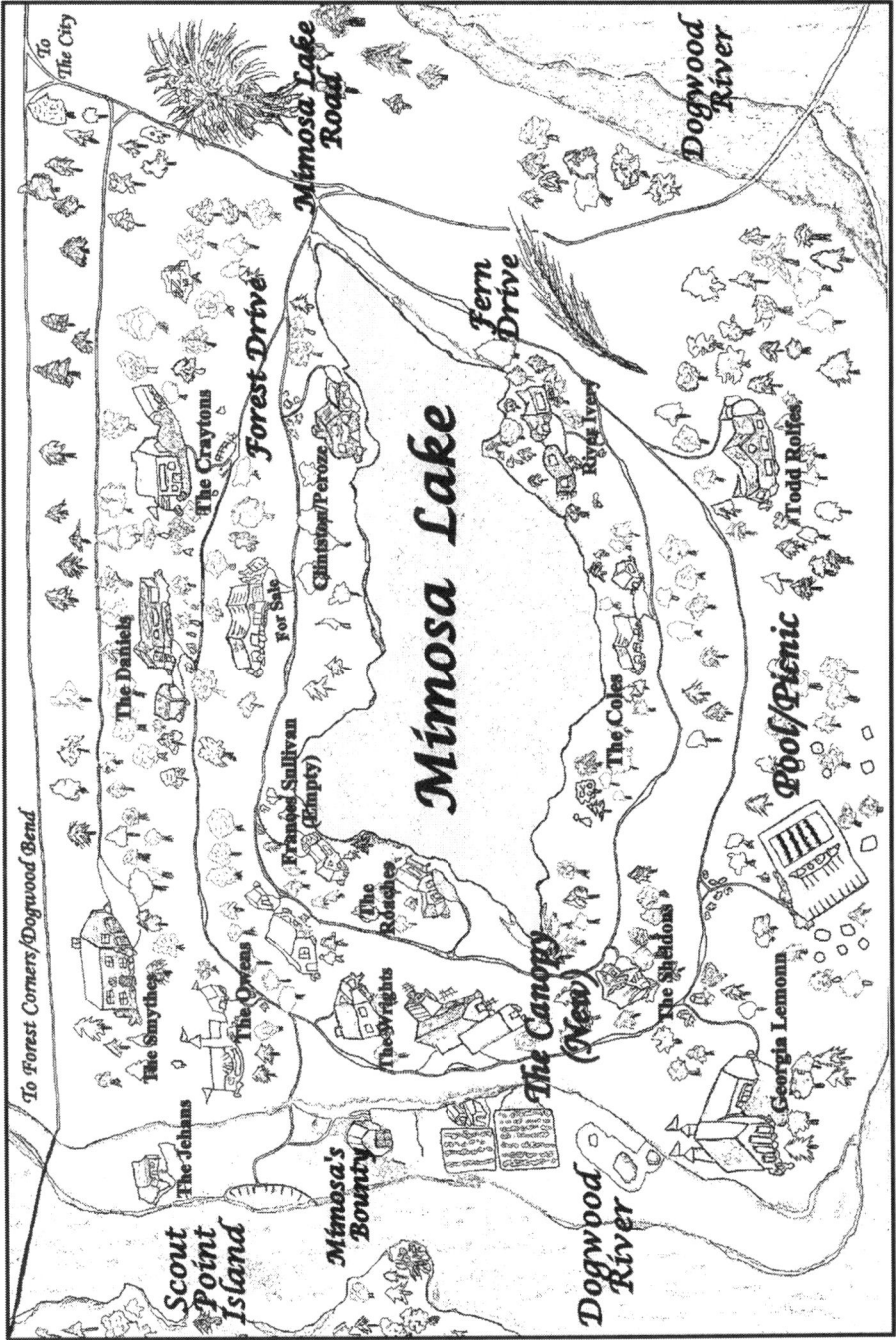

Mimosa Lake

To The City

Dogwood River

Dogwood River

Mimosa Lake Road

Fern Drive

Forest Drive

The Craytons

Johnston/Peroze

For Sale

The Daniels

Frances Sullivan (Empty)

The Roaches

Todd Rolfes

Rick Ivers

The Coles

The Shadons

Pool/Picnic

The Smythes

The Owens

The Wrights

The Canopy (New)

Georgia Lemons

To Forest Corners/Dogwood Bend

The Jehans

Scout Point Island

Mimosa's Bounty

Dogwood River

To find other books (in this series or others) by K.S. Wuertz, order additional print or electronic copies of *Christmas at Mimosa Lake: Angels on High* to contact the author visit:

www.kswuertz.com

Cover Design and Illustrations by K. S. Wuertz

First Edition: October 2015

Created and Published in the USA, KSWuertz Publications

Library of Congress Cataloging- in- Publication Data

Wuertz, Kimberlee S.

Christmas at Mimosa Lake: Angels on High/Kimberlee Wuertz – 1st Edition

ISBN: 978-1517269654

Christmas at Mimosa Lake: Angels on High

Angels on High

No Foot is Struck

-1-

River Ivery was finally heading home to Mimosa Lake. The trip had been a long one. She'd taken the Jeep and followed her paintings to shows from Chicago to Milwaukee to Minneapolis. Thad had warned her against driving in early December but she'd felt the need to get away. Sugar, the boxer mix she'd inherited from her neighbors the Potts, lay in the front seat snoring. The music played softly, it helped her to remain a relaxed driver.

The shows had been good and the gallery opening in Minneapolis had been fun! Thad had flown up for it and was so gracious as she made her way around, meeting all the patrons. Her life was fulfilled in so many ways. A snort from Sugar brought her attention back to the road and out of the clouds.

"Time to stop, girl." She petted Sugar's head. Sugar chuffed in response. Sugar was a talking dog. She always had the last word, it was just part of her boxer nature. "Ready for a break?"

At the question she sat up and perked up her ears. "Roooo, Ruff, ruff," Sugar chimed in.

"We're about 15 minutes to the next town." River answered as she drove on. The day was clear and the air was cold. A storm had been through the day before, but the roads were mostly clear. Soon she'd be off the interstate and onto the back roads that would take her toward Mimosa Lake. They were two hours from home, but the hilly area around the rivers might be a challenge.

She put it out of her mind as they stopped to gas up and take a break.

"Did I hear you tell him you're goin' on down 29?" A trucker asked who opened the door for her on her way out of the truck stop.

"Yeah, that's where we're headed." River answered.

"Well, there's a slick spot or two. I came up that way from Dogwood Bend 'bout 3 hours ago. Be careful, ya hear." He tipped his cap to her.

"Thanks, safe travels." She responded. *'Way to raise my anxiety.'* She thought.

"Well, Sugar, we'll just take it slow and steady." River picked up her cell and hit Thad's picture.

"Almost home, beautiful?" He answered.

"About three hours. But I heard the roads may be slick." She sighed.

"Why don't you stay on the interstate and come in here tonight. Go out tomorrow?" He offered.

"Mmmm... I want to get home. I'll see how it is and turn back if I have to." She paused. "You understand?"

"Sure honey, whatever you want to do. I'll be out tomorrow." He answered.

"O.K. I'll call you when I get home, or later tonight. Love you." She tried to sound cheerful. She'd stayed an extra day in Minneapolis with friends just to avoid the weather. Maybe Thad had been right, traveling in winter. Of course the Jeep had 4-wheel drive. River reached down to turn it on and changed her mind. Once she got to 29, she'd stop. "O.K. girl. Let's do it."

The sunshine sparkling on the snow was so beautiful it raised her spirits. She wondered how the cats were. Tim Cole, her

2

trustworthy neighbor had been keeping an eye on 'the Boys', and the house when Thad wasn't there.

River yearned for the quiet of her studio and the smell of her paints. She'd be in there by tomorrow this time, unpacking some new materials she'd gotten in Milwaukee and Minnesota. God willing.

River could hardly wait. And Christmas was coming! Her parents would fly in and she'd have a chance to show off the engagement ring Thad had designed for her. In January, the plans for their wedding would take center stage. They'd be married next May.

The road raced by and Sugar shifted in her seat. River turned up her CD. They flew past the sign: Hwy 29 / 5 miles. At the top of the ramp at 29, she stopped and put Sugar on her leash. They took a walk around the Jeep and over into the brush alongside the road. Sugar took the cue and had a bathroom break. "Good girl, Sug." River walked her back up to the Jeep.

She put the Jeep in 4-wheel drive and drove onto 29. It wasn't as bad as she'd imagined. The only thing on the pavement was water. All that worry for nothing, even into the woods the water trickled across the road. River took a breath of thanks. Soon, she'd cross the Dogwood for the first time.

The Dogwood River snaked through the south east part of the state. The hills surrounding the Dogwood rolled deep into woods, then over huge vistas where the river valley could be seen, blanketed with fresh snow.

She slowed on the curves in the high hills, but when she hit a high plateau that was brilliantly lit with sunshine, she stepped on the pedal. The Jeep surged and then began to spin.

"Whewwwww!" She steered to correct herself taking her foot off the gas. Sugar cried in fear. It all happened so fast, the ditch was coming toward them and they were down an embankment before she knew it. The Jeep jolted to a stop, tossing Sugar against the dashboard and to the floor. River was belted in, but she banged her head on the steering wheel.

She sat for just a minute, trying to take a breath. Then she felt a trickle of blood run from her forehead. The engine was still running, so she turned it off.

"Sugar? Girl?" River felt for her.

Sugar cried in response, jumping up on the seat and licking her. River grabbed her and held her. "Thank God, you're O.K."

She reached in the console for the box of wipes and swung the mirror around. Just a small cut above her left eye. She dabbed at it and it stung. Her first aid kit was way in the back. "Buried when you need it." She said. Sugar shook as she snuggled against her.

River took off her seatbelt and looked around. There was a large pine tree about five feet away. Had they hit it and then been thrown back? She opened the door. Sugar jumped out ahead of her.

They walked around the Jeep. Everything looked alright. The embankment was at least fifteen-foot tall. She'd never drive out of here. River scooped up some snow and held it against her forehead. The cold stung, but maybe it wouldn't swell as bad.

She walked back around to the driver's side of the car and reached in for her cell phone. She tapped, and tapped again – dead.

"Great." Only then did she realize how shaken up she was. She felt weak and wobbly. "Don't panic, it gets you nowhere." She coached herself. Sugar licked her hand in affirmation.

"You O.K. down there?" A voice said from somewhere above.

"Hello?" She walked around the back of the Jeep and looked up the embankment. "Hello. Yeah, I'm alright." She called up to him, relieved.

4

At the top of the hill, stood a man in coveralls, his white hair stuck out from beneath his hat. "Looks like you got a good bump on the head. I'm a gonna throw you a rope and you tie yourself 'round the waist. I'll pull you up."

He didn't look strong enough to pull her up. "Are you sure? I'm O.K. if you want to go for help." She offered. No use both of them getting stuck.

"Take me almost what's left a daylight to get to town. I'll manage." He threw the rope down. "I'll have my son come get your car out later. Come on."

River took her backpack out of the Jeep and put it on. She looked at Sugar, who was jumping and wagging her tail. "I can't leave my dog." She called as she tied the rope around Sugar.

"I got 'im." The man pulled a surprisingly calm Sugar up the hill. "'K. Your turn, Miss." He threw the rope back down and River tied it around her waist three times.

"I'm ready." She looked up and said a prayer. "Please Lord, will you help us? I don't want him down here."

With surprising strength she felt herself being hoisted up the hill. She tried to grab footing in the snow as she went but he pulled her up so quickly.

He offered his hand to her and pulled her the last way over the hill to the gravel. "There we go." He said with a breath.

"Oh! Thank you!" She said with relief. "Thank you, Mister?"

"Smith, Tom Smith." He tipped his cap, reminding her of the truck driver and his warning. He smiled. "Now, we cain't get your car out till my son comes home, so you might as well com' on to th' house. Mother's got some dinner waitin', one more ain't gonna matter. That's gonna be a shiner ov'r that eye. Mother'll get ya fixed up."

River had her reservations, but she was stranded. She reasoned she could outrun him or Sugar would bite him if anything went wrong.

"I'll do ya no harm, Miss." He said, as if in response to her thoughts.

River shook her head. "Thank you for your kind offer."

He motioned to his tractor, parked on the road. "Climb on up right there." He pointed. "Think you can hold on?"

"Yeah. Thanks." River climbed and Sugar jumped onto the floorboard. "Is she O.K.?"

"Yep." He sat down on the bright red tractor seat and started the engine with a roar. The tractor jerked forward. They rolled along, River wondering where they were going. Nothing looked as familiar. Maybe it was the accident.

"I don't know where we are." She yelled at him.

"29, headin' home. Turn off to the house is right 'round this bend." He pointed as they bounced along. Sure enough, a long gravel road ran alongside an open field. "Mother's waitin' dinner, hope you're hungry. We'll get you fixed up."

River bumped along, Sugar looking out across the field. She held onto the back of his seat. The air smelled like sugar cookies, but when a bump in the road jostled her toward her rescuer, she realized he smelled like sugar cookies. She had to smile.

"Right yonder." He pointed a gloved finger toward a frame house that sat at the edge of the woods down the road, overlooking the field. Smoke was winding up from its chimney into the cold air.

He pulled the tractor to the bend in the driveway near the back porch door. "Hand me that there, will you?" He pointed to a bell on a rope hooked onto the bottom of his seat. River handed him the bell and he rang it.

6

It wasn't a minute before a short, rounded woman appeared at the door. Her eyes were so bright and kind, River could see them from down the sidewalk.

"Mother, we got a stranger for dinner. She ran off the road up yonder by Two Forks." The old man said. "Might need some attention from your medical bag.

The woman wiped her hands on her apron. "Must be shaken with fear. Oh! Look at that gash on your forehead! We'll get that fixed up in no time. Come in, come in." She opened her arms to River.

Sugar, having no need for protocol or manners, jumped off the tractor and ran to her. She jumped on her skirt and barking with delight.

"Sugar!" River got down as quickly as she could. "I'm sorry." She apologized over her shoulder as she stepped off the tractor. Then looking at Mr. Smith she said, "Thank you,Mr. Smith. You're a God-send."

"A course!" He smiled.

"She's O.K., child." Mrs. Smith laughed. River walked toward Mrs. Smith, she felt so welcomed. What else could she do?

Franklin Sheldon was enjoying his walk today more than usual. His daughter Ellenour was visiting from upstate. She'd come in just two days ago, before the storm.

"I never get tired of walking the roads around here." Ellenour walked alongside her father who walked along, puffing his pipe and tapping his cane on the hardened snow of Forest Drive. They were in the woods just about to come to Pastor Jack and Nakita Daniels' place which sat above them, on the hillside.

Nakita was outside, loading baby Grace into her car seat. She waved and smiled. "Good morning, Professor. Ellenour!"

"How's Grace?" Franklin inquired from the bottom of the driveway.

"She's wonderful. Four months tomorrow." Nakita beamed with joy.

They waved and went on.

"You know Dad, she looks so happy. I'm happy for them." Ellenour smiled.

"Was a long time coming." Franklin smiled. "But children, like all good things are worth the wait. What about you?"

"Was I worth the wait?" Ellenour asked, avoiding his obvious question and referring to their sorted history. Ellenour was the result of a brief affair Franklin had over 30 years ago. They'd found out about Ellenour's lineage only after her Mother's death a little over three years before. The news had almost broken up Franklin's marriage. But eventually, Beverlee Sheldon had accepted the situation and now looked on Ellenour as the daughter she'd never had.

"You were more than worth the wait. I wish there'd been none." Franklin shrugged. "Life's got a funny way of giving gifts."

"Yep." She put her arm through her father's as they approached the Crayton's home. Dock was up the ladder, hanging lights.

Dock Crayton was a man of perfection. He liked his yard, like his house, like his person – immaculate. The Crayton's dogs, Princess the shiatsu, and Duke the German Shepherd, were outside helping.

When Dock went to the pound last Christmas to get Trixie a dog for Christmas, he fell in love with them both. So, he came home with two dogs. Trixie Crayton had jumped for joy.

8

"Got some good help up there, Dock." Franklin commented from down by the mailbox as he reached down to pet Kaiser, who had run down the driveway to meet him. "Here boy." He said, handing him a treat from his pocket. All the Mimosa Lake dogs knew Franklin. They waited for him to walk past.

"Couldn't do it without 'em." Dock took his cigar from his mouth as he climbed down the ladder. "This one's waitin' on Trixie to get home." He motioned to Princess who was running around on the deck by him.

"Moved down here yet?" He called to Ellenour.

"We finish school two weeks school and then we'll move over Christmas break." Ellenour answered.

"I guess we'll let 'em come on down, right Dad?" He asked Franklin.

"Can't wait!" Franklin raised his cane and they walked on.

As they crossed the dam, two eagles soared above them. The brilliant sunshine sparkled on the cold, dark lake. Ellenour took her hat off for a moment and let the wind blow through her hair. It felt good, crisp and tingly.

"How are River and Thad?" She asked.

"Doin' well. Getting married sometime in May or June. Guess they'll beat you to the altar." He tapped along. "River should be back soon. She's been gone since right after Thanksgiving.

"So they set a date. Great! They're getting married at the beginning of the summer, we're at the end." Ellenour walked along, noticing Franklin was beginning to limp a little more. "Let's slow down, Dad." She slowed the pace as they rounded the bend toward home.

"We're almost home. I'm fine." Franklin tapped along. "No, I'm better than fine, Daughter." He puffed on his pipe, holding it in his teeth as he spoke.

If Tim Cole wasn't seeing it with his own eyes, he'd never believe it. He blinked to make sure the sun wasn't playing tricks on him. Nope, she was still there.

The most brilliant and lovely woman, stood down by the arching oak tree, near where River's dog, Rue was buried. He watched her from inside River's front door.

It was close to noon, maybe the light was just sparkling on the water, casting shadows. But then he heard her sweet voice inside his head.

"Good tidings of great joy! Behold, you are loved by the most high. Alleliuah!"

Her words filled his heart and for the first time in over a year, he felt no pain in his body – or his soul.

He was too mesmerized to respond. A tear trickling down his cheek distracted him. He was embarrassed to be so emotional. Tim wiped his face with the sleeve of his coveralls. Then looked out at her again, but there was nothing there.

"A dream?" He said to himself before he was interrupted by Thomas, River's hungry cat. "Yeah man, I'm comin' right now."

He started to turn away, but looked back, expecting to see her. Nothing.

Thomas gave him another reminder – this time at a higher pitch. Tim went across the dining room and behind the long bar that faced the living room and front of the house. He grabbed one of the cans of cat food and a dish from the stack River had left on the counter. Thomas was very insistent.

The rest of 'The Boys' as River called them, came out of their hiding places and encircled Tim. He felt like a chef in a Sushi bar. Finally, he placed four dishes, out and the room got quiet as everyone concentrated on eating.

Wolfman, Tim's trusty sidekick waited for him just outside the front door on the patio. Is someone had been there, Wolfman would have gone to investigate.

"Just a mirage." Tim said aloud and shook his head. He put on his hat and pulled his long, greying ponytail out from under it.

The deep blanket of hopelessness, lay back down upon him. Tim was a broken-hearted man living in a broken body. Pain surrounded him. But like all good-hearted souls, like all souls, God has plans for Tim Cole.

Peggy Owens put on her sweater vest with the Angels holding bells on it. The tiny bells were sewn just above each button hole, so she 'rang' as she walked. Bridgett, her Maltese and Taffy, the stray she'd rescued three years ago, danced around her as she walked through the house to get the doorbell.

"Here you are!" She opened her arms to her friend Charity. Charity helped her buy their first bike from 'Hog Wild', the Harley store in Dogwood Bend.

Biking had not only reignited her marriage with Alvin, it had brought them to the CMA, the Christian Motorcycle Association. And, it had been the basis of friendship for Peggy and Charity, who led two very different lives.

Charity had been a 'biker chik' and Peggy, a middle-aged, overweight, rigidly-Christian, woman who was tired of her life – including her husband.

Now, Peggy was more relaxed and Charity was going to church with them. The Lord does work in mysterious ways.

"Do you like it?" Charity asked, as she took off her hat. She'd dyed a bright pink streak in blonde hair.

"It gives you some holiday sparkle." Peggy smiled as she took her friend's coat.

"Nick likes it." Charity followed Peggy and the dogs to the kitchen.

"Alvin's Christmas cookies are on top of the stove. What do you want to drink?" She asked.

"Coke." Charity answered. At 28, she could still drink soda and eat cookies with no effects.

They settled in the living room for girl talk. Nick was being Nick. Peggy wasn't that fond of him, but she said little. She knew Charity would find her way. This was the third boyfriend she'd lived with in as many years. Charity had no family to speak of and Peggy played the role of surrogate mom or sister, depending on the topic of conversation.

"So I don't know where I'll be by Christmas. With things so bad at the store, I don't have much cash to rent a place of my own." Charity looked down. "Why do I always end up with these losers?"

"You have certainly kissed your share of frogs." Peggy agreed as she petted the sleeping Taffy on her lap. She was silent a minute. "Why don't you move into the little apartment out back by Alvin's shop?" She'd offered before she'd really thought about it. "Of course, we'd have some rules."

"I don't know, I don't want to lose you as a friend." Charity looked away.

"You think about it and I'll talk to Alvin." She said.

Right on cue, Alvin walked in the back kitchen door with Harry, his blue tick heeler in tow. He was home from working at the Canopy.

"Hey Hun, 'm home." He called.

"In here, Charity's here." Peggy answered.

"Hi Hun," He kissed Peggy's cheek and waddled over to Charity on the couch. "Good to see, ya." He said as she reached up and hugged him.

"'t's cold out there, gals. Sun's gone down. Got 'vrything put 'way up there. Ready to bake 'n the mornin'." Alvin took off his coat and hung it in the hall closet. Harry plopped down in front of the fire.

"I've got to get going. Nick gets home in an hour." Charity stood up.

"Don't 'et me break ya up." Alvin replied. "I'm changin' clothes and goin' out ta th' shop."

"No, no. I need to go on. Thanks Peggy." Charity took her coat and put it on.

"See you Sunday?" Peggy asked.

"Sure, sure." Charity smiled, gave Peggy a hug and stepped out into the cold. She looked back to the end of the driveway, to the little apartment that was attached onto Alvin's shop, then turned around to look over Mimosa Lake which lay below her.

The lights were coming on around the neighborhood. It was dark early these days. Eagles circled above her and headed east, flying over the newly-built Canopy, the Mimosa Lake community center. They flew on up over the bluff and she imagined over the Dogwood River below the cliffs, then to Scout Point Island to their nests.

She took a deep breath, "It's so lovely here." Her words added to the white in the cold.

13

Entertaining Angels
-2-

He was one of the biggest men she'd ever seen. He had to be at least six and a half feet tall. River stood as he walked into the room, half ducking under the archway. Mrs. Smith didn't even look up from her sewing.

"Call me Mrytle," She'd said to River over dinner.

"Mrytle?" River said as she stood.

"This is our son, Michael. Michael, Miss River Ivery. She's gotten her car stuck up yonder by Two Forks. Went down the hill, almost hit a tree." Myrtle's rocking chair squeaked as in rhythm with her words.

"Miss Ivery." Michael extended his large hand, enveloping hers in a gentle handshake.

His touch made her feel... joyful. "I'm happy to meet you, Michael. Your parents have been so wonderful to Sugar and I."

"Daddy told me where you're stuck at. I'll go out there in a minute. Just came in for a sandwich, Mama." He kissed his Mother on the cheek and went toward the kitchen. Sugar following his every step. "Come one, little one." He said to her.

River sat back down on the sofa near Mrytle. You have been so kind. I won't impose on you much longer. I'll ride on up there with Michael, if you don't mind."

"I mind." Michael had returned with a sandwich in hand. River noted that for a man so large, he made very little noise.

"Michael, mind your manners." Mrytle warned him, even though it was obvious he was in his late twenties or early thirties.

"Ma... Miss River, it's startin' to spit ice outside. That's why I'm in such a hurry to get your car down here. No use you riskin' it tonight. It'll be slick."

"Oh Son, I hadn't heard." Mrytle rocked away, but she put her sewing down a minute and took off her glasses. She smiled at River. "Guess we'll put sheets on the spare bed."

"Oh, I couldn't stay. Maybe we should look at the weather report on TV?" She asked.

"We don't have one." They chimed in together.

"No reception down here in this valley." Michael added. "I been listenin' to the radio for the forecast." He finished his sandwich and stood up. "Mama, I'm gonna get Daddy outta the barn. We'll be back before dark."

"I'll have supper ready." Mrytle smiled at her son. "River, will you help me fix somethin' you can eat?"

"Sure." River said. She felt defeated. She was so ready to get home. And what about Thad?

"You're worried about getting home? And your fiancé? Is that what's on your mind?" Mrytle asked.

"You read my mind, Mrytle." River said with a smile. "I don't want Thad to worry. But I know no one drives on ice. It looked so clear when I started out this morning. I thought the weather was going to be good all day." River shrugged her shoulders. "Never know."

"Never know around here. Let me see if Michael can get word to your fiancé for you." She got up and went out the back door.

Sugar laid at River's feet. River looked around the well-kept room. The oval rug covered the polished wood floor. The bookcase was filled with books. The glass on the lamps shined, not a speck of dust anywhere. A colorful afghan covered the back of the couch, and brightly needlepointed pillows accented the furniture. It was a bit old fashioned, but homey.

The kitchen was warm from the wood stove in the dining room that heated the whole first floor. River heard the kitchen door open and close.

"River, what's his phone number?" Micheal called from the kitchen. "Sorry, can't come in to get it. I got my barn boots on."

River went into the kitchen. "Here it is, she took a pencil from the buffet in the dining room and a piece of paper from her backpack. "Better yet, here's his card." She reached down into a pocket in the backpack and pulled out his card. "Thank you so much, Michael."

"Yeah, Mama and Daddy aren't much on the outside world. But don't worry, I'll let him know you're OK. Anything you want me to tell him?"

"Just that I'll be home as soon as I can." River felt a little better, knowing Thad wouldn't worry.

Michael met his mother at the door as he left. She was carrying a pile of sweet potatoes in an old rounded bottom tin bowl. "Got these from the cellar." She reached in her big apron pocket and pulled out two glass jars. "Green beans and pickled beets."

"Yum..." River rubbed her hands together. "Sounds good."

"I tell you child, cooking will get your mind off of all your troubles." Mrytle laughed. Her laughter sounded like bells ringing. "Wash up and let's get to it. I'm gonna make my buttermilk cake tonight, we'll celebrate you comin' to visit, River."

As the afternoon waned, the ice tapped at the window. River could see by the light that it had slickened up. Mrytle brought her a cup of tea and sat across the kitchen table from her.

"They'll get that car of yours home and in the barn 'fore too long. You a worrier, River?" She asked.

Her eyes were so kind and warm, River didn't take offense. "I try not to be. I think worrying denotes a lack of faith. But..." She rolled her eyes, "I know I worry more than I mean to."

Mrytle smiled. "Now that's a good way to put it! I worry more than I mean to." Her tone turned serious for a moment. "That's not what our Heavenly Father would want His faithful disciples to do."

"Yeah, we're all a work in progress." River looked around the yellow kitchen, towels hung neatly drying near the warm oven, the checked tablecloth and woven placemats, complete with cloth napkins and even the African violets that bloomed on the cart by the window against the dark gray, icy afternoon. "I'm so grateful Tom found me and brought me here. That's what I'm going to think about, Mrytle."

"Oh! Take a sip of tea and let's get upstairs and fix your bed. Bring your backpack, you might want a bath before dinner." Mrytle took another sip of her coffee. "You know River, the work is never done around here. But it's good work."

"I know what you mean. I love working in my home, too. God has blessed me so many times over, Mrytle." She took the last sip of tea.

"As He does us all, child." Mrytle picked up their cups and put them in the sink. Then she led the way upstairs, Sugar following behind.

Each evening, just about dark, Herbert Potts had taken to walking again. Before his wife Selma left, he used to walk to escape her. That's when they had their dog, Sugar.

But Selma had even given the dog away when she'd gone to Seattle to live with their daughter Anna, and her partner Sharon. But Herbert refused to think about that. Their ways were ungodly and he'd have no part of it. Anna was dead to him.

Herbert didn't miss Sugar much. She was an unruly misbehaved animal. Better that she was with 'Crazy River' across the lake. She'd be about right for that kind of a dog.

The sliver of sun remaining on the horizon was a brilliant red. December stars were filling in the sky as the light receded. Somehow, his footsteps always brought him here.

He stood in the driveway of the empty blue split-level house. The 'For Sale' sign sat crooked in the yard, bent and propped up yet again the wind. Its condition almost foretold the shape of the property it represented.

Herbert looked up at the windows, remembering the rooms, but mostly remembering the owner: Randi Kepter. To this day Herbert remains convinced, God meant them to be together. He still holds out hope that someday, Randi will see things his way- God's way.

It had been almost a year and a half since Randi had gone to prison. She'd burned down the Canopy two years ago and she'd burned down some buildings in Ohio before she'd moved to Mimosa Lake. Herbert knew she didn't really mean to do it. She just needed help. Well, they hadn't helped her much.

Randi Kepter was not a common criminal like those other people in prison. It was torture for her. He could see it when he went to visit her. Sometimes she wouldn't even see him. Herbert knew, she wasn't rejecting him, just trying to protect him from the pain of it all.

There was no chance she'd be out for at least eight more years. Herbert had to wait. What else could he do? Then, he imagined, they'd move far away from here.

He walked up around the back and looked at the back deck. Inside the sliding glass doors sat a kitchen table, Randi's kitchen table. The deck had patches of ice on it, but his prints were the only prints in the snow. He looked up the hill. He could see Pastor Daniel's lights and Dock' lights further on down the road. Dock's place looked all lit up, warm inside.

Herbert was cold and getting colder, but sometimes he stayed here longer. All he had waiting was TV and the TV dinner to go with it.

He walked down the driveway and turned toward home. When he got to a clearing by the lake he looked up. Why had God forsaken him? All he'd done was try to follow the Word. God wouldn't have brought Randi to him, if it wasn't meant to be.

A righteous man doesn't question God. He quickly averted his thoughts and walked on toward home.

The house was quiet in the early afternoon. Grace Elizabeth Daniels lay asleep in her crib in her cool, darkened room. Nakita Daniels had a few minutes to herself. She went to the kitchen table and carefully unwrapped the package from California that her mother had sent. She opened the box to the most beautiful angel with dark hair and a little gold halo. She carried a sign that hung from a piece of gold and white cord from her hand that read: *Grace's First Christmas.* Tears ran down her face as she held the little angel. She'd call her mother when she calmed down.

Nakita thought she'd stop crying after she'd had Grace, four months ago. Then came post-partum depression, which really wasn't depression for her. Instead, everything touched her heart so deeply. Now just watching her child sleep or after listening to her coo, or when she'd started to laugh two weeks ago: it all touched her heart at the core.

Christmas was Jack's busiest time at the church. And soon, their parents would all be here for Grace's first Christmas. Nakita felt like heaven truly had touched earth. Her cell phone buzzed on the table. She quickly wiped the tears from her cheek and picked it up.

"Hi Hermey." Her nickname for her husband, who resembled the elf in *Rudolph the Red Nosed Reindeer*.

"Nick, I'm coming home early. Everyone thinks there's going to be ice this evening, so no Trustees meeting. Do we need anything in case we get iced in?"

"You could get us some milk and another package of diapers. Oh, I need two packages of broccoli for the rice dish I'm making tomorrow." She answered.

"Have you been crying again, honey?" His voice suddenly softened.

"No... Yes... Mom sent the most beautiful little angel for Grace." She answered. "I'm O.K."

"Let's get the tree put up tonight, the one in the living room. You up for it?" He asked.

"Sounds great. I've got vegetable soup for supper, so come on home." She perked up at the thought. They'd get the live tree for the back porch next weekend.

"Nick, we have so much to be thankful for, don't we?" He asked.

"We do. I love you, Hermey." She answered.

"Be there soon. I love you, too." He hung up. Pastor Jack Daniels buzzed his secretary, Amy Graeser. "Amy, it's time to head home. Pick up those boys early and get home safe."

"I didn't hear the weather was bad. I heard no snow till Saturday." Amy didn't stop typing as she listened for him.

"People are talking about ice tonight." Jack was standing at her doorway. Amy jumped in response. "Sorry," he said.

"Really?" She put her hand to her beating heart. "Are you leaving, too?"

"Yep. Nothing moves on ice. Except the Spirit." Jack laughed.

"I'm so disappointed, no Trustee's meeting." Amy smiled, then she spun around in her chair and met his eyes. "You don't think they'll reschedule it, this month, December Do you?"

"Merry Christmas, I got us out of it for the month." Jack laughed.

"I shouldn't sound so...well... like I sound." Amy replied with a bit of guilt.

"No need to explain, just get home safe. Now pack up and let's get outta here!" Jack went back to his office to get his laptop and what he needed. Within ten minutes they were gone.

The Tree of Life Methodist Churchsat empty in the mid-afternoon gray. Soon ice pellets would peck against the stained glass, sending echoes through the house of God.

River opened her eyes to the sunlit room, white light reflecting from the snow and the last of yesterday's ice. The long icicles on her window were already dripping their way to the ground two stories below.

"Sugar?" She spoke as she smelled the coffee and bacon. Bacon can still smell good, even to a vegetarian. Sugar stretched at her feet and jumped off the bed.

River got up and made the bed, pulling the wool, tied quilt up over the fluffed pillows. She quickly changed into her jeans and long sweatshirt. She'd be alright until she got home.

She slipped on her socks and shoes and opened her bedroom door into the large foyer at the top of the stairs. Across the foyer was the bathroom. She stopped for a minute to freshen up and then went down to greet the Smiths.

"There's our guest." Tom Smith was finishing up his breakfast. "You sleep till noon every day?" He laughed, teasing her.

"I heard you get up. What time was it?" River asked as Myrtle handed her a cup of coffee.

"Cows like to be milked at four. That's what they need, so that's what we do. Right, Michael?"

Michael nodded as he took another pile of bacon onto his plate. "Mornin' River, how'd you sleep?"

"Oh... I slept like a stone. It felt great. It was almost like being at home." She smiled. "I'm surprised I slept so well, after my great defeat in Scrabble last night!" She laughed.

"No one beats me in Scrabble." Michael said as he took the syrup to a fresh stack of pancakes that Mrytle put on his plate.

"You being an artist and all, we thought you might get creative with your words, River. You almost had him toppled once or twice." Tom commented with a teasing smile.

"You two leave poor River alone! Considering the day she had, it was good of her to stay up and play at all." Myrtle stepped in to defend River amidst their laughter.

River got up to get another cup of coffee. "Thanks Myrtle, us girls have to stick together." River gave her a quick hug.

23

"Mother, come sit down. You too, River. Your breakfast is gonna be cold." Tom took a sip of hot coffee River poured him as she poured round the table.

They all sat down. "Time for a prayer." Tom's voice became solemn. They joined hands. "Lord, we thank you for bringing River our way. We've enjoyed the time we had together. Thank you for the food before us and all the goodness you provide in life. We ask for Godspeed to River as she goes on home today. Amen."

"And..." River chimed in. "Thank you for these wonderful people who saved me from the cold and warmed my soul with your love. Amen!"

They ate and talked about the farm and River's travels. Sugar was given two eggs and a half plate of ham.

"I guess she's eating my part of the meat." River chimed in when Michael sat his plate down for Sugar on the floor. She wagged her tail in thanks.

"Rooo...Roof...Ruff...Rufff!" Sugar commented.

"Now Michael, you can drive River to the highway, won't you son?" Tom asked.

"Sure, Daddy." Michael answered. "I'll follow you River, just to make sure you get out O.K." He laughed. "Who knows, she may get stuck again and have to stay till spring!"

"I don't think so!" She smiled. "But, Myrtle, Tom, Michael, when you're coming to Dogwood Bend again, please let me know. Thad and I would love to have you out to the house. Please do come," River offered.

"We usually don't get that far, but we'll see you again. I'm sure of it." Tom answered as he smiled at Myrtle with a knowing look.

24

River helped Mrytle with the dishes as the men brought the Jeep out of the barn and warmed it up. Sugar ran around outside as the sun warmed the winter air.

"Mrytle, how can I ever thank you and your family? You've been so kind. I feel like an undeserving stranger." River dried the last of the pots and set them on the counter for Mrytle to put away.

Mrytle's bright blue eyes softened, as if she was in thought. "River, you just pay it forward. You can do that." She emptied out the dishpan and wiped it down with her cloth. "You never know in the morning what the day's gonna bring. Yesterday brought us the blessing that only strangers can bring when they knock on the door, the blessing of new friendships." She smiled.

"River..." Michael called. "You're ready as you'll ever be."

"O.K." She called back. She picked up her coat and took one last look at the little house. "I hope Thad and I have the kind of marriage you and Tom do. I'm going to tell him all about you." She smiled.

"Godspeed, be safe on those roads, River." Myrtle gave her a tight hug. "Oh! I packed you an apple butter sandwich. There's bacon in there for Sugar and here's some fruit. And the left over buttermilk cake."

"It's a good thing I'm not staying, I'd never fit in my jeans." River stepped outside in the crisp air.

Tom wrapped his big strong arms around her. "You take care little girl." He smiled.

"Thanks again, Tom. I don't know how you found me down there so quick." River frowned at the thought.

"It was the Lord's will." He smiled and his dark eyes twinkled.

Michael was on the tractor seat. River and Sugar got in the car. Michael followed them down the long lane that had a few slick spots where the sun hadn't hit yet. When she got up the gravel road to 29, it was clear. She stopped the Jeep and hopped out.

Michael jumped down off the idling tractor. "You'll make it from here, River." He held out his hand.

She took his big hand in hers and felt that familiar warmth. She felt a surge of confidence and hope. "Michael, you have been so much help. I don't deserve your kindness. Thank you so much."

"You just get home to Thad in one piece, ya hear?" He smiled.

"I will. See you again, soon, I hope." River waved and climbed into the Jeep. "Let's go, Sugar." She turned onto the road and left Michael waving at the end of the drive.

She made it across the bridge on 29 and through Leonard's Landing. The small town sat just on the above bluffs of the Dogwood as it winds through this part of the country. Within an hour she was nearing Dogwood Bend and her phone was working. She left Thad a message as she sailed through the sunshine toward Mimosa Lake.

What had once been a bare island, devoid of human activity was now housing monitoring equipment for weather, water and wildlife. But the eagles didn't mind.

They seemed to know, it was to their benefit that a few humans crept around the place. The Dogwood had flowed around Scout Point Island almost the beginning of time, certainly longer than man had rowed his boats around it. It would continue to flow, and provide fish, whether humans watched it or not. He knew this, instinctively.

There were now 14 nesting pairs on Scout Point Island. It was becoming 'eagle central'. This brought humans with strange glasses to the Dogwood River Bridge and to the island itself in summer.

On this winter afternoon, equipment was being moved around at Mimosa's Bounty, the organic farm just across from the south east shore of Scout Point Island. Jacob Latcher was moving the tiller to the front of the new barn in preparation for winter wheat planting. The tractor chugged along, filling the area with puffs of smoke and noise, but it kept all eagle eyes entertained.

A crew from the university was on the island, checking equipment and downloading recorded stats before they reset the machines.

He called out to the world before he spread his wings and circled to the highest of heights. His eye caught the Jeep below, just as it turned onto Mimosa Lake Road. He followed it as it turned onto Fern Drive and then into the driveway that led to the arching oak tree where he liked to sit. He glided and circled around to the tree and landed atop the arching trunk. It was his way of welcoming her home.

Message: Delivered
-3-

Frances Sullivan's death was a blow to all at Mimosa Lake. She'd died suddenly in August, leaving part of her estate in question. River was appointed executer of the will.

River could still hear Frances' soft voice as she read the words. Frances, would always be known as a wise and kind-hearted woman.

River knew that Frances had endured years of suffering when her husband Woody was alive. Woody was a mean drunk, and he'd been drunk most of the time. Frances never spoke of him, after his death. Her kind demeanor and way of standing up for the downtrodden was already missed at Mimosa Lake. River thought about all the times Frances had reached out to her, during the 'Canopy mess'.

River and Georgia Lemonn patched their friendship up after the accusations of setting fire to the Canopy were dropped against River. Intellectually, River knew Georgia had been in a bad position, as president of the MOB (the Mimosa Lake Organizing Board). But in her heart, she still felt pangs of betrayal.

Georgia avoided River during that time. Before then, River had thought of Georgia like a surrogate mother. And now, more like a fair weather friend. Though she realized that was unfair, it was how she felt. It was an issue she took to God in prayer – daily.

This morning, River readied herself to put her stamp of approval, or disapproval on the decisions that were made as per Frances' request. She was meeting Dock, Georgia and Peggy Owens at the attorney's office in Dogwood Bend.

The drive there was beautiful. The snow sparkled and the roads were clear. She couldn't help but think what a wonderful week it had been, even her slide off the road up on 29 had brought her to the Smith family. What a joy they were! She couldn't stop thinking about them. And tonight, Thad would be home She missed him more than she ever thought she could miss anyone.

"Hello everyone," Robert Hathers brought his large folder into the room followed by his secretary. Robert was known as the best estate attorney in Woodland County – and beyond. "River, do we have a settlement?"

"I'm counting on them, but more important, Frances is counting on you." River smiled at Dock, Peggy and Georgia. "God Bless her."

"Yes, God Bless her." Peggy smiled back at River.

"As you know, Mrs. Sullivan's children did not want the house at Mimosa Lake. Her valuables have been distributed to her children and the Raptor Society according to her wishes, with the exception on the home." Mr. Hathers took a breath. "Maggie, pass out the transfer of deed information to them, will you?"

Maggie obliged her boss' instructions.

"Now, as per Mrs. Sullivan's request, the property at 45 Fern Drive, Mimosa Lake is to be distributed to a deserving party as determined by the executor, River Elace Ivery along with Mrs. Georgia Lemonn, Mrs. Peggy Owens and Douglas 'Dock' Crayton. The property is to be distributed, according to the Trust, no later than six months after the death of Mrs. Frances Sullivan."

Mr. Hathers stopped for a moment and looked at them all with seriousness in his eyes. He reminded River of Atticus Finch eyeing the jury. "Technically you have until February 4th, but a decision made now, will save the estate paying taxes on the property next year. River?"

"As the executor of the estate, I'd like to request the names of the possible candidates you have to occupy the home." River looked at Georgia but it was Dock who spoke up.

"River, there's only one name we want to submit." He eyed Georgia and Peggy, as if they might change their minds before he spoke.

"And that is…" River coaxed him on.

"Mallie and Joos Jehan." Dock answered.

River had to admit, she hadn't thought about the Jehans. "I hadn't thought about the Jehans, but I can see why they would be a good choice.

"Who were you thinking about River?" Georgia asked.

"Todd had crossed my mind, he's bumping around in the big house all alone. Also Jake and Emmabella, they just got married. But I believe you've made the best choice. Do you think the Smythes will mind?" She asked.

"I don't think so, they can have their little boathouse back. They'll always be Emmanuel's grandparents, no matter where they live. And it's just up the hill." Peggy said.

River turned to Mr. Hathers. "Robert, I think we've decided. Frances' home will be given to the Jehan family." River announced, then turned to her friends. "Frances would be so happy."

"Alright. Let's see Maggie, this is the 8th already. How soon can we get the transfer completed?" Robert Hathers looked over his glasses at his secretary.

"When will you notify the Jehans? They may not accept the offer." Maggie, the voice of reality, struck them.

"She's right. They'd be crazy, I'd never look a gift-house in the mouth." Dock broke up the room.

"Mr. Hathers, will you get the expenses on the house together for the Jehans?" River asked. "Can we set an appointment for Monday to meet back here?"

"Why wait? Why don't we just go see them River? Then they have the weekend to talk it over." Peggy offered.

"That's what we'll do. But still, get the expenses on the house together, will you?" River was persistent.

"Will do." Maggie gave her a knowing look. "We'll arrange to meet here on Monday… 10:30? If that works for the Jehans."

Everyone agreed. They would go see Mallie and Joos this evening.

With eagle eyes they looked down at the little boathouse that sat on the Dogwood River bottoms. Its lights lit up the coming evening. A few more circles around the sky and it would be time to roost.

The female called to him, and in the distance he heard the cries of the other eagles, returning to Scout Point Island after a winter's day of fishing and searching for food. A deer had died down river and a pack of coyotes was finishing off the carcass. He flew above, watching them tear and pull at the flesh.

He caught a lift higher in the air and flew just above the trees on the bluffs before he circled toward their nest that sat on the southwest cliffs of Scout Point Island. He cried as he landed and they stood together in the deep nest, sheltered from the cold.

Mallie Jehan loved her son, but today he was every bit the two year old he was about to officially become on his birthday next week.

"Emannuel! Mommy told you not to get into the kitchen drawer. You will pull it out on your head." She'd picked him up, screaming and kicking, just as her husband came in from work.

"Here Mal," Joos held out his arms to his son, who reached for his father. What's going on buddy?" Joos asked his exasperated wife.

"I want it! Why…. Why…." Emmanuel sobbed as the phone started ringing.

They looked at each other, remembering their agreement. Joos smiled first and then Mallie threw her hands in the air and went for the phone. When life was crazy, remember the good stuff. It's a simple rule, one that many forget.

"Well, that was River. She wants to stop by right after supper. Can you give him a bath and I'll finish in here." Mallie looked at the disheveled kitchen as the phone rang again.

"Hi honey, we are bringing pizzas out from town. Don't cook." Victoria Smythe, aka adopted parent/grandparent to the Jehan family was on the other end of the phone.

"Oh….." Mallie sighed. "That would be great. The kitchen is a mess, Manny has been all over the place today." She sounded as tired as she was.

"Perfect. We'll be there in about 20 minutes." Victoria clicked off.

"Now, you promise NOT to TELL THEM." Victoria looked at her husband out of the corner of her eye. "I know it will be hard."

"I promise, my dearest." Chef Elmont Smythe's words were drawn out by heavy French-Canadian accent. Victoria knew, this was a sign of deep thought.

"Elmont, they aren't ours to keep. Children are all about moving and changing. They are about life." Victoria comforted him. Elmont was a very emotional man, who had fallen in love with the Jehan family when they were brought to Mimosa Lake by chance, two years ago.

"Yes, yes... They'll only be up the hill. But will they need us any longer?" He asked, almost not expecting an answer.

"Of course they will need us. Manny is only two." Victoria took a wisp of her blonde hair and stuck it under her felt hat. "Besides, I think the day is coming when our family might expand."

This attracted Elmont's attention and brought him into the present. "What? What? What has she said? Is there another baby coming?"

"No... nothing yet. I can just tell, it's on their minds. So you see, if another baby came, they'd have to leave the boathouse and move. Maybe even to Dogwood Bend." Victoria had accomplished her goal, her husband could see the good in it all.

"Yes. Yes... this way, they will just be at our beloved Frances'. Ahh... Victoria, yes. This will be a very good thing. How wonderful Frances was, to think of such a thing!" Elmont sped on ahead to get to their pizza dinner.

After pizza was over, the neighbors came down with their offering to Mallie and Joos. The couple sat silently, taking in Frances' generosity.

Finally Joos spoke. "So they don't want us to pay the house off?" He asked again in disbelief. "Why us?"

River explained again Frances's wishes. "Let's give you the weekend to think it over. The attorney in Dogwood Bend will have all the financial and legal information you need on Monday." She finished.

"I realize this is a big bomb we've dropped – even if it's a good one." Dock added. "Take some time to wrap your mind around it. Frances wants her house to be left in good hands, you two can handle it."

"We will talk about it." Elmont assured them.

Dock stood and everyone took the cue. "It's been a long day."

"It sure has…" Mallie said, as she went to their bedroom to get their coats off the bed. "Thank you so much. It's an honor that you've even thought of us."

Joos stopped her and put his arm around her. "We didn't even know you two years ago. You've given us a place to call home." Wise words from such a young man.

After the goodnights were said and the little boathouse lights all turned off. As always, they laid in bed together, listening to the sound of their two year old asleep in the crib at the end of the room.

Joos began. "Thank you for my son and my wife."

"Thank you for the loving people who are trying to help us." Mallie followed.

"Thank you for the new house." Joos spoke it, because both knew the decision was made.

Because really, who can look a gift house in the mouth?

Harris saw her first. Lucinda was down the next aisle looking for a new IPad for Samantha, their ten year old.

She looked as if she was lost, so much so that his eyes followed her. Her cart was full of shoes, coats, 2 blankets and a few groceries. She abruptly turned down the aisle in the back and pushed out of sight.

He went back to weighing the features of two HD TV's. They needed a new one for the downstairs den. Years of Jake hanging out with friends and watching movies had taken its toll on the old set. Now that Jacob and Emmabella were married, and living away from home, he could safely replace the old one with something he wanted.

Well, at least they were safely away most of the time. Jake had stayed over some nights during harvest, the drive in and out of Dogwood Bend was getting to him. Plus, Jacob was meant to live in the country. As he'd told Lucinda many times, they 'd work it out. Harris returned to the 72" set just as Lucinda came around the corner with the boxed IPad.

"If we can just keep it hidden until Christmas." She lifted it in the air for him to see. "I got the last one!"

"Or maybe the day after, just so she'd think it wasn't coming. You know, more of a surprise. No. I can't stand to hear the word 'IPad' come out of her mouth any more times than necessary." Harris laughed. "What will she want when she's 16?"

"Everything." Lucinda laughed. She pushed the cart ahead and turned around. "Is it TV time?" She asked.

"Not today, sweetheart. Just looking." Harris smiled. "Let's rock. River and Thad are probably already there."

"Yeah, I'm hungry for the Limp Noodle's lasagna." Lucinda pushed the cart to the front of the store.

Harris noticed the woman he'd seen earlier ahead of them in line. She carefully laid all of her items on the checkout and stood back. Children's clothes and coats, shoes and groceries, but not too much.

"$312.17" The cashier said.

"Oh, oh… I need to put something back. Are you sure? I was adding it up …." The woman was flustered.

"I'm sure." The cashier looked at Harris and rolled her eyes.

It angered him and he stepped up. "What's wrong?" He asked.

"I thought I had enough. I'm sorry to hold up the line." The woman apologized. "I was trying to get something for all of them…"

"How much is it?" Harris asked again.

"312.17" The cashier's voice was much kinder now.

He took out his credit card and handed it to her. "Use this." He held his hand up to the woman who was digging in her purse to offer him cash.

"Merry Christmas." He said to her.

She began to sob. "I don't know what to say. I just don't have enough for everything and my boys are cold without coats. Thank you."

Lucinda put her arms around the woman. "I understand, I've been there." Her words were broken between her emotion and her Mexican accent.

"You are good people." She thanked them again and again before she left.

"Thank you, darling." Lucinda was proud of him. "I love your heart the most of all."

As they left, they saw the woman sitting on the bench outside in the cold with her cart. Lucinda immediately went to her.

"Do you not have a car?" She asked.

"No, no..." The woman was crying. "I am just so overwhelmed. Earlier today, I wondered why I should go on. I lost my job as a secretary about four months ago. I can't find anything." She took a tissue Lucinda handed her and wiped her eyes, then pulled her sweater more tightly around her. "Now, I know God is telling me something."

Harris reached in his pocket and pulled out his business card. He also pulled out $300 and folded it all neatly together. "This isn't because it's Christmas. This is because you need the help. Take it, and call me next week. Maybe we can find you something in my company, if you're qualified."

With a shaky hand, she reached up and took what he offered. "Do you believe in angels?" She asked through her joyful tears.

Harris and Lucinda smiled.

"You would do the same for us, if things were different." Lucinda hugged her tight. "God bless you.... I don't know your name."

"Mary." She smiled. "My name is Mary."

Jet Wright followed his master down the road into the Mimosa River bottoms. Most of the fields of Mimosa's Bounty, the organic farm run by Jacob Latcher, lay fallow for winter.

'W' Wright, Missy Wright's middle child and only son, walked ahead as Jet roamed the field and woods nearby. W's father,

Carl, had been killed going on three years ago during a snowstorm when he slid off the bridge that crossed the Dogwood River just north of where they were walking.

Jet, a handsome, black German Shepherd often walked with W to the area where Carl's truck had been found. Somehow, W took comfort in seeing the site. Even he didn't know why.

But today, they turned in the opposite direction. Walking along the river, directly across from the southern tip of Scout Point Island. The eagles flew above them, dipping occasionally into the water for a fish. W loved to watch them dive.

"Come on, Jet." They followed the river as it rounded the bend beneath Georgia Lemonn's large home that looked like a castle sitting high on the cliffs above the bottomland.

Soon they were on the back road by the farm that curved past the southwest fields of Mimosa's Bounty and up to edge of the woods. That's when W saw her, the most beautiful woman standing at the edge of the woods. She was filled with brightness and had the most beautiful sparkling eyes. Her smile drew him closer.

"Your prayers have been heard." She said, but W noticed she didn't move her mouth.

"Huh? How?" He asked. "What prayers?" He wasn't afraid, more curious. Jet was down sniffing along the river, far away.

"Your prayers for her." She smiled kindly and W knew then.

"My mom's a good mom. But she's so lonely." W answered.

"God bless the son who loves his mother." She held her hand up, opened-palmed toward the sky, but just for a moment.

W's gaze followed her opened hand to the sky. It seemed so bright, but only for a moment.

"God bless you, too." W answered, before he could even think what to say. Jet barked and he knew he'd seen the woman. "It's O.K., boy." W called to him.

Then turned back to her. Her eyes met his and he felt so warm inside. But she faded from him as he watched. Where she had been was only a wet clump of snow-covered grass and a dark tree trunk. W Wright knew good things were about to happen.

Fury of White
-4-

Firecracker Stew was what was needed, Alvin Owens decided. Usually a content man, these days Alvin was particularly happy. The Canopy had been rebuilt into an even greater facility than before. That Thadius Sandberg knew his stuff.

Alvin had helped design the kitchen. Of course Chef Elmont Smythe and his assistant were there every step of the way. Alvin loved being here. The only place he loved more was being in bed with Peggy, or maybe on a motorcycle ride with the CMA. No matter, Alvin was in his element.

He worked around the kitchen, shuffling from place to place. He put dishes in the dishwasher, pulled out the big new stewpot from under the counter and got into the knife drawer. Periodically he stopped, he'd almost swear he was bein' watched. Alvin shook it off. "No one here." He muttered. He took the meat from the fridge to get it ready.

"No use cuttin' more vegt'bles 'till the meat's cooked up. He poured oil into one of the big pots on the stove and turned up the gas. The flame licked the bottom of the pot, heating it quickly. Too quickly.

Oil had dripped down the side. Now, a small flame crawled up the side of the metal toward the top, threatening to go down into the vat of hot oil. But almost magically, the flame extinguished, saving the pot, the oil, the Canopy and Alvin Owens.

Only the smell of gas made him turn around. He waddled back over to the pot. The oil was hot. He looked around and found a rag, carefully wiping off the bottom and sides that were blackened by the flame.

"B'tr be caref'l." He mumbled to himself, as Tim Cole walked through the doors into the dining room followed by his beloved dog, Wolfman. The new kitchen was fully open into the dining room, only separated by a long bar.

Alvin was safe now, she faded from the corner where she'd carefully watched over him. Alvin Owens was a man with problems like anyone else, but on earth, and in heaven, he's known as one of the good ones.

Emmabella Mayer Latcher listened closely to her friend's voice on her cell. "I think I'd better come over, Mallie." EmmyB was known as the voice of calm, even amongst the twentysomething set at Mimosa Lake. "I'll come after one, when you get him down for nap." She hit the screen and clicked off.

"What's going on?" Her mother-in-law asked from the other room.

Emmabella quickly recounted the story about Frances's house to Lucinda.

"Frances' was truly a generous woman. And her children agreeing to it. What a great tribute." Lucinda concluded.

"I guess Frances left them a lot of money, who knew?" EmmyB smiled. "I'm so happy for Mallie and Joos."

Jacob called from downstairs, but two floors up in the main offices of Mimosa's Bounty all they heard was his voice. EmmyB went to the top of the stairs. Her husband stood below, on the first floor landing, bathed in sunlight from the skylight that lit the stairs. She loved everything about him, even that pout that he was wearing.

"EmmyB did you hear me?" Jake sounded perturbed. He looked up at her, his long, black thick, ponytail hung out the back of his cap.

"No. What's up?" She asked.

"Someone's made a camp upriver and left three dead deer. I'm going to get the tractor and dispose of them. Will you call Mike Plant?" Jake asked his wife. Mike Plant was the area conservation agent.

"Sure. Want some help?" She asked.

"No, W Wright wants to go with me. We'll be back before dark." Jake stomped back toward the door. There was a poacher in their midst and Jacob didn't like poachers. "Later…"

Emmabella returned to her desk and rang the Conservation office. She'd work until time to go to Mallie's for lunch.

"All the talk at Loli's is about a big storm that's coming on Wednesday night." Trixie Stokes Crayton told her husband amid the clamor of cooking supper in their kitchen.

Duke, Dock's German shepherd mix, and Princess, Trixie's Shiatsu were underfoot. Ever since Dock had brought them home last Christmas as a surprise for his wife, they had disagreed on how to discipline the dogs.

Trixie, of course, felt sorry for them because they'd been shelter dogs, mistreated in her mind. They deserved everything they wanted, including sweaters, extra treats, endless toys and bones and the Dog channel on satellite.

Dock, was the disciplinarian. He knew a good dog knew his place in the pack. He'd watched enough of the Dog Whisperer to know that. Consequently, Duke was much better behaved than Princess.

43

Duke was Dock's constant companion. Princess spent her days on the sofa in the den when Trixie was at work and on Trixie's lap every evening.

"Princess, you have to move away from Mommy's feet." Trixie's pink high heels clicked on the kitchen floor. "Here, have a bite of Daddy's steak."

"Whoa!" Dock responded. "You're gonna make that dog fat, honey."

"Oh Dock, look how tiny she is. Here Duke, you need a bite of steak to keep those bones strong." Although Duke could have taken Trixie's small hand off up to the elbow, he gently took the piece of steak from her. "Now, I'll give you the bone if you're good." Duke's large tail beat against the floor in response.

Dock didn't know what had happened to his house. But he knew this: never, had he loved coming home as much.

River cleaned up the last of the dinner dishes and put them in the dishwasher. Thad was in the shower and Sugar was on the couch snoring. The cats were in their usual spots. It seemed darker outside tonight than other nights. She looked through the row of ceiling to floor windows across the front of her earth home that overlooked the woods and Mimosa Lake beyond. But tonight, she could barely see the patio furniture sitting outside.

Her eyes rested on Rue's picture hanging on the wall above the dining room table across the room to her right. Every time she looked at it, she still missed Rue, her beloved husky was gone for over three years now.

Thad appeared in the doorway, with a towel wrapped around his waist. "Honey, we're out of that oatmeal lotion for my skin. You know, the stuff you have made in Dogwood Bend." He dried his blonde hair with a smaller towel as he spoke.

44

Thadius Sandberg was a man of few inhibitions, she loved that about her fiancé. He was himself, no matter where or when.

"River? Honey? You thinking about the Smith family again?" He asked.

"No, I was actually thinking about you." She smiled.

"Oh, well, come over here and think about me some more..." He swiveled his hips at her.

"Wooooo!.... You are a treat for the eyes Mr. Sandberg." She played with him.

They met midway for a kiss. His back was still damp. "Aren't you cold?" She asked.

"Not anymore." He went in for a deeper kiss and she responded. "I missed you. Boy, did I miss you." He muttered between kisses, as he steered her toward the bedroom.

An hour later, Sugar rousted from the sofa. The house was quiet, but all the lights were on. She explored her dish in the kitchen and chomped down the few last morsels she'd left earlier, then she followed their voices, wandering into the bedroom.

"It's not that I haven't met kind people in my life. My life's been filled with good people." River twisted her head around to meet his eyes as she lay in Thad's arms. "You're one. You're one of the best, Thad."

"But...." He urged her on.

"But there's such a fullness of life that they have. I just don't see very many people who truly understand life and live it big. I don't mean big, like for attention. No, big... like being sure to make every minute count." She was lost in thought. "They're so thankful – and happy."

"I'd love to meet them sometime." Thad replied.

"Would you? Would you really? Because I was thinking…" River started.

"When? When were you thinking?" Thad asked.

"Well, after this storm, if it comes. And Thad, I'd like to get them some Christmas gifts. But I can't think of a thing they need." River laid thinking in the low light that shown into their room from the bathroom.

"You said they look like they come from another time. Would they like a TV or something like that?" Thad asked. "I mean, something…new?"

"No, it doesn't really fit them. Thad, isn't it strange to find people who live so simply… and they're the ones who have it all." River thought about the Smith's simple two story frame house, about the woven rugs on the floor and the quilts Myrtle made on all the beds.

"I hope that we can be that happy after all those years of marriage." Thad yawned and it brought them back to reality.

"Are you going in tomorrow?" She asked.

"Yep, at least until the weather gets bad. If the storm even comes. I'd better get an early start." He kissed her and reached for the alarm clock that was on her side of the bed. He set it, then put it back.

She wrapped her arms around him before he could lay back down. "I hate to even think about you going away when you just got here." They held each other for a long time. He began to fall asleep against her.

"You rest, I'll lock up." She kissed him on the forehead and got up. "Come on Sugar, let's get you outside girl."

She left him to sleep while she watched the ten o'clock news.

The tree was big for their little apartment, but it cheered the place up. Emmabella scooped the chili into their bowls and Jake grabbed a beer from the fridge.

"Milk for you?" He asked, his back to her as he bent into the refrigerator. "I'm getting out the cheese and onions."

"Yes, milk for me. I don't know how you can eat chili and drink beer in the middle of the night." Emmy laughed at her husband.

"It's only 10:30." He kissed her and then loaded down his bowl with cheese, onions and crackers. "Mom's chili?" He asked.

"Of course. You hate my mom's chili." She answered.

"Not hot enough." He sat at their little dining room table. Neither of them offered to turn on the TV. Emmy had lit the candles.

"It's a beautiful tree, Jake. Do you think it'll live?" She asked as they sat together.

"It has enough of a ball on it. I dug it up over a month ago, it shows no signs of stress. Yeah, it'll be fine." He finished his bowl of chili and returned to the kitchen for another.

"Jake, I saw Mallie today. Do you know about the house?" She asked him.

"I heard, great for them. They were stretching the boathouse. Manny's getting bigger, more toys." Jake sat back down. "Emmy, great chili. Just like Mom's." He dove into the bowl.

They listened to the rumble of a large truck pass by on the street downstairs. Emmy sighed. "City living."

"City living." He replied. They both hated it, but it was what they could afford. "It's not so bad. You're here." He smiled at her and winked.

"No, it's pretty good." She leaned over and kissed him. "Chili breath!"

"We'll find a house of our own, Emmy. Maybe next spring, after first planting." Jake offered.

"I'm happy for them. But I can tell, they are blown away." Emmy picked up her bowl and moved into the kitchen. "I wonder if Felicia and Malkirk know about it."

"Sure, Felicia's at Georgia's. Mal is coming out this weekend for the hayride. They know. We'll have to help them move." Jake took the last bite of chili. "Ahhhh…that was great. Now, what about that cake?"

"Jacob, I made it to take to your Mom's tomorrow night." Emmy protested. "Have some of these cookies instead. Sometimes, I think you're a bottomless pit."

"Food and sex." He winked at her. "How about it?"

"What about it?" She smiled softly. It had been hard to wait until they were married, but Emmabella was glad they had, it had been worth the wait.

"Christmas is coming early, huh?" Jake came up behind her and put his arms around her. As he kissed the back of her neck, his ponytail fell on her shoulder. She turned around. "You're so easy." He laughed softly.

"So are you." She smiled at him. "Merry Christmas, again…"

It started with a few flakes. It always does. As with anything, there is a beginning and an end. Georgia Lemonn stood on the

48

hillside, watching the snow come in, knowing that they'd make it through another storm.

She'd already called Dock and had him bring extra supplies to the Canopy. The extra refrigerators and freezers had saved them a couple of times, not to mention the generator. Now, all she could do was wait for Felicia to get home.

Amanda, her helper and companion tapped on the kitchen window, breaking her thoughts. Amanda opened the kitchen door. "Are you lost in the snowstorm already?" Amanda's round, cheerful face was always a comfort to Georgia.

"I think you should go on, if you're leaving." Georgia replied. "I'll be alright until Felicia and Malkirk get here." She worried about Amanda. Georgia felt obligated to worry for the selfless souls of the world. Amanda always put others first. Secretly, Georgia wondered how she did it.

"You mean I can't have one of the spare bedrooms?" Amanda asked, knowing the answer.

"Of course. If you want to stay." Georgia's tone lightened. She somehow felt safer with people around these days.

"We have some serious baking to do before everyone comes. Christmas is only a little over two weeks away. What better time to bake than in a snowstorm?" Amanda almost chirped at the thought. "I'm making lunch. Egg salad and tomato soup in about 15 minutes."

She shut the door, leaving Georgia to the wind that was picking up. It was at times like these that she missed Plato the most. Her treasured cocker spaniel had died last winter. Mr. Mittens, her cat still wandered around the house still looking for him.

Georgia walked on down to the grove of pines near the bluff. Below the bluffs lay Mimosa's Bounty and the Dogwood River. Today, the river had a dark gray cast to its rolling waters. The eagles circled and dove through the whitening sky. She knew they were preparing. How did they know without weather reports?

She walked along the ridge and back up toward the gardens that lay on the soft slopes near the north side of the house. Amanda and Georgia had spent a day last fall cutting back the rose bushes and harvesting the last of the squash before her yard man came to plow under the remaining garden.

It all was in order. Georgia liked order, but life has a way of creating chaos, like snowstorms.

"I thought I'd make it out in time, but the roads are just getting worse. Luckily, I ran across Dock at Loli's, I'm gonna follow him." Thad's voice sounded tense. "Do we need anything, River? The roads are treacherous."

"Just you to come home. I went shopping this morning before I came over here." River was at work in the studio, which was warmed by the fire. But she had the television on, watching the weather. "Thadius, come home darling. If you need to leave the car at Loli's, she won't care. Ride with Dock." She knew it was wasted breath. There was something about men and conquering weather she had yet to understand.

"No, I'll be fine following Dock's truck." Thad nodded at Trixie as she sat a cup of hot coffee down in front of him.

"Closin' up!" Loli announced to the five diners left at the Lumberjack Café. "Got to get home, all a you should be leavin' too."

Trixie whispered to Dock, who nodded. Then she went to her boss.

"You all need to get outta here. Do what you can for clean-up. I'll stay and load the dishwasher." Loli announced to the kitchen

50

cooks. "What is it, honey?" She turned to Trixie. "You need to go ahead to get home, go on."

"No, we want you to come out to our place. No use you sittin' in town alone. Come on, we could use a good breakfast in the morning." Trixie thought of Loli like a mother.

"Awwww… I don't want to bother you and Dock. You got to have some time alone now and then. Snowstorms can be romantic." Loli lifted her eyes.

"Pack up your gear, we ain't leavin till you come with us. We got a caravan going out there, with Thad followin'. You girls can ride with me and Duke in the truck." Dock's voice boomed across the room. "Let's get a move on, it's comin' down." His warning was timely, as the lights of a snowplow flashed through the front windows of the café.

"You heard the man, lockin' up." Loli went to the back. Trixie went to the cash register.

Within twenty minutes, they were loaded up. Loli grabbed three cartons of cigarettes, enough for almost a week and an extra change of clothes she kept for emergencies.

Thad was behind them, wishing he'd taken River's jeep this morning. Dock started out. The road had just been plowed, but it was covered again. Thad was guided by Dock's lights.

There is a knowing that comes with living in a remote place. Like city dwellers adapt to tall buildings and ever-changing stoplights, those who live in the country tune themselves to the ways of nature. The adjustment often comes with a battle, sometimes many battles, but finally the lesson is learned: it's just better to work with the ways of the nature.

Thadius was still battling, but he was learning. His fingers gripped the wheel as the car slid down the hills of Mimosa Lake Road. The ditches seemed deeper – and steeper - than he'd noticed before.

51

Dock picked up the pace a couple of times, the roads were no problem for him with the 4-wheel drive. But he'd slow up and wait for Thad.

The trip to Loli's was 20 minutes on a clear day, but it was an hour and a half until they pulled into the Mimosa Lake development.

Dock stopped at the split of Fern and Forest Drives. The Craytons lived up the hill on Forest Drive. River lived across the dam on Fern.

"You be able to make it across the dam?" Dock yelled to Thad out the window.

"I'll make it. Can't thank you enough." Thad raised his hand and waved them off. Trixie and Loli waved back.

"Careful now." Dock added, as he turned to the left to head up the hill.

Thad drove slowly across the dam and on around. River's trees and the little purple studio, nestled amongst them never looked so good to him. He pulled in the driveway and hit the garage door opener.

River opened the inside garage door as he pulled in. Sugar ran round the car barking. He clicked the opener and the door rolled back down.

"Damn!" He got out of the car and went to his fiancé's open arms. "Never again."

She held him tight, but leaned back and looked at him for a minute. "You've learned."

"I have." He replied.

Today, Thadius Sandberg had become a wiser man.

Heavenly Voices Lifted
-5-

Alvin Owens wasn't cooking breakfast at the Canopy this morning. He'd tried to get down their long driveway and given it up. The snow was still blowing and drifting. It had turned the world of white upon white.

Peggy Owens awoke to the smell of bacon and coffee. She knew she'd have to call her girls at Its Your Business, the Forest Corners job placement agency she managed. No one would be interviewing today.

Peggy padded into the living room in her favorite pair of pajamas, the pink ones with the 'Hello Kitty' heads all over them. She was enthusiastically greeted by Bridgett and Taffy, and eventually Harry who sauntered out of the kitchen. The dogs knew a day at home when they saw it.

"Mornin' Hun." Alvin's back was to her as he cracked the eggs into the skillet. "Just 'n time." He added.

She kissed him on his round cheek. "I've got to call everyone so they don't come in."

"N't much chance 'a th't. Roads closed, 'ven the hi'way." He poured their orange juice as Peggy got a cup for her coffee. "L'ks like 'ts me 'n you taday, Hun.

At the Clintston/Peroze household, just down the hill at the other end of the lake, Samantha Clintston was on her IPhone. There was no school today, but that didn't stop middle school social life.

"Can't get to the farm with the road closed." Jacob Latcher told Emmabella over breakfast in their little apartment.

She could tell, he was going to get antsy. "Black Ops Two? I'll light the tree." She offered.

He looked out the window and sighed. "Sure." He smiled. And she could see the child in her husband for a moment.

It was just another day to Herbert Potts. He didn't pay much attention to anything or anyone. In the silent house, he got out his bowl for oatmeal. He put it in the microwave and waited for it to ring. The coffee pot perked, the red light flashed letting him know the morning coffee was done. There was no place to go and nothing to do.

He sat at the kitchen table and ate. For some reason, the day that his daughter Anna told him she was a queer came to his mind. It was at this table where she so brazenly spoke up against him and the Lord. He went to strike her for her blasphemous words and works, but her queer roommate stopped him. Herbert remained convinced that Sharon had turned Anna queer. She certainly didn't leave home that way. Now, Selma, his ex-wife was living out there in Seattle with them. "There's things a lot worse than being here." He spoke to no one as he shook his head.

River and Thad were watching the news. The smell of coffee filled the great room that housed the kitchen, living room and dining room of the earth home. Outside the snow was piled on the patio furniture, covered with a tarp for the winter. The solid heavy board that served as a flat feeder for the birds was drifted with snow.

Still, the cardinals, bluejays, nuthatches and a variety of finches flew in and found their food. The woodpeckers were at the peanut butter logs and occasionally a Cedar waxwing thrilled them with its presence.

"I left my briefcase in the car. What's on your plate today?" Thad asked over a bowl of granola he'd retrieved from the kitchen.

"Finish the order for the Hamilton Foundation in Minnesota. I think I can ship it next week, if I push through." River looked at him over the rim of her coffee cup. His hair was still tasseled from sleep and his eyes revealed his age first thing every morning. But oh, she loved him.

"I need an office here. I'm going to draw something up." Thad announced.

"O.K. But will my office work for today?" She asked.

"Sure." He nodded as he crunched his cereal. After breakfast, they would all brave the elements and trudge across the driveway to the little purple house that served as River's studio.

Tim Cole was about to take Wolfman out for his walk when he felt a strange catch in his leg. "Ahhh…." He bent over with the pain.

"What you cryin' about in there?" Teresa Cole called from the living room.

"Just got a pain in my leg." He rubbed on it and it subsided. Tim felt his age more than he ever had. His brief affair with Kalista Riner last year had made him feel so young and alive. It was as if he'd stepped out of his life for those few months. He had no regrets. But once it ended, it was as if he saw his life for the first time. And he didn't like it.

Wolfman ran out the door and Tim stepped into the cold and swirling snow. The snow had quit falling for the moment, it was just shifting with the wind. He shuffled through the snow, off the deck and around the house.

That's when he saw her again, standing by his workshop up the hill.

"All will be as it's intended. Rejoice! The Lord is near!" He heard her words so clearly in his head. He felt uplifted. For a moment he was filled with joy. It felt foreign to him.

As Wolfman ran up the driveway, Tim kept his eyes on the beautiful woman who sparkled against the snow. He stepped on his leg and there was no pain. Then, unexpectedly, Tim Cole began to cry.

It had taken a couple of days, but things were back to normal. The roads were open and everyone in Woodland County and well beyond was in the Christmas spirit. It's an added advantage of December snow.

Thad and River started out early that morning to go up north to see the Smith family. River's jeep would fare the long lane to the Smith's house better, so they bounced along after stopping at Loli's for an early morning breakfast.

They turned onto Highway 29 and crossed the bridge, driving up into the hills toward the interstate. But they'd made it almost to the interstate before they turned around. River couldn't find the Smith's lane.

"I'll find it on the way back. It'll be easier to spot coming from this way." She assured Thad, and herself. Thad drove slowly. "Here's where I went in the ditch, see that tree." She pointed down.

"Wow..." Thad looked as he kept his eyes on the road. "How did he ever pull you up outta of there?" They drove on. Down the hill, around the curve by the trees and the field opened up to the right of the road.

"I thought the field was plowed under." River shrugged her shoulders. The fence seemed more broken down. "I must have been in a brain fog from the accident." She was thinking out loud. "The road is right there." She pointed to a barely visible lane that ran along the south side of the field.

"Looks risky, but we can make it." Thad turned down the road. "Guess they haven't been out since the storm." He commented on the unplowed road.

"Is it too deep?" She asked as they bumped along.

"No, I'll just keep moving. Maybe they'll run the tractor over it before we leave. They rolled on down past the field and wound up to the farmhouse that came into view. But it didn't look as welcoming as River remembered.

Finally, they were in the yard. The back porch screen door was hanging on one hinge. But there was something else, the house was dark.

"This is the place?" Thadius asked with trepidation. "Maybe we took a wrong turn."

"No, no." River got out in the sunshine that was melting the bits of snow off the sidewalk. "This is it. The house is here, there's the pump, the barn is over there and the tractor shed is..." She looked around. There was a big white lump where the tractor shed had stood.

A chill ran up her spine, but she steadied herself. "Thad?" She walked up to the porch and through the screen door. The door to the kitchen was locked. It looked like the kitchen hadn't been used in years. Everything was filled with dust. On the back porch was a broken down ringer washing machine.

"Thad..." She called to him as he looked around over by the barn.

"River.... There's no equipment in here. I don't think this barn's been used for anything but hay storage for quite a while." He walked toward her.

"Thad, the kitchen looks right." She peered through the windows on the back porch further into the house. "There's the

57

door to the dining room, and back there goes into the living room. Look, the rug is right there on the dining room floor."

"I don't know. Are you sure this is the right place, honey? Farmhouses can look alike. Maybe we didn't go far enough back down 29 toward town." He looked in the window behind her.

"I know this is it. Where could they have gone so fast? It's only been two weeks. This place looks like it hasn't been lived in for over twenty years." She was frustrated. "I have to find out where they are."

"Well they aren't here. Let's take a stab at going on down 29, maybe there's another road." Thad tried to comfort her. "Whatdaya say?"

"Yeah, there's nothing here. Was there anything in the barn?" She asked.

"Only some hay bales and a red tractor seat." Thad replied.

"A red tractor seat?" River's voice lilted. "Red? Thad, Tom Smith had a tractor with a red seat."

"So do a million other farmers, honey. Besides, that one is old." Thad headed for the car, only to find River running through the drifts of snow toward the barn. "Honey…" He ran to catch up with her. He was convinced they had the wrong place. People don't abandon a farm in two weeks and leave it in this condition.

"Thad! I know that's the right seat. See the holes in it?" River was encourage. "How could they abandon this place in two weeks?" The wheels were turning.

"Let's check out the roads closer into town." Thad suggested.

"O.K." River walked back toward the Jeep and the house. It all looked right, except the fallen machine shed.

Thad followed their tire tracks out the long lane and back toward Highway 29.

58

"Don't stop here or you'll never keep the momentum to get onto 29 from the driveway." River warned.

"Not even married yet and you're back seat driving." Thad mumbled under his breath.

"Hey, watch it Mister!" River's voice mirrored her excitement. "I know we're close to finding them."

They bounced up onto 29 and headed south toward the bridge and Leonard's Landing. Thad drove slowly, but there was no other field with a road beside it on the right hand side of 29.

"You sure you didn't turn left?" Thad asked. "Like into that road over there?" He pointed.

"No, no... I know we didn't come this far on the tractor and look, there's a blue sign there: Cossa's Blueberries. I would have remembered that." She watched closely until they came to the open fields of the bottomlands. The bridge lay about a mile ahead. The road rose up the man-made embankments that kept 29 from flooding.

"Thad, that's the only place it could have been. Let's stop in at Mayfair, that's the local hangout up here and see if they know what happened to the Smiths." River suggested. "I really wanted to give them the painting before Christmas."

"We'll find them, I'm sure. Remember honey, I got a call from them saying you were alright. It's a small town, they can't be that hard to find." Thad pulled into the diner parking lot. "Luckily, it's the lunch rush, so someone will know where they've gone."

When they walked in and were seated at one of the front booths, they got the looks that every stranger gets when he or she enters a small town eatery. The waitress was soon over for their order.

"Before we order," River began, "We were looking for the Smith family who live off of 29 up north. Their place looks empty. Do you know where they've gone?"

"The Smith Family?" The waitress knit her eyebrows together. "I've never heard of them, let me ask in back after I get your drinks."

River and Thad quickly ordered and were left to listen to the loud conversations of the other diners. Out of the inaudible roar came a question that caught River's ear.

"Who wants to know about the old place off of 29?" The male voice asked. The waitress pointed to their table. With a scrape of the chair across the wood, he was on his feet. The wooden floor squeaked as he walked across it. River thought it odd that she could hear it above the noise of conversations.

"You folks askin' about the old Knettly place up off a 29?" He held his hand out to Thad, who shook it firmly.

"Yes sir. Maybe, I can tell you how the lane looks that goes down to the house and barn. My fiancé, River, just spent a night up there with a family named Smiths about two weeks ago and we've come to thank them." Thad offered him a seat.

He pulled up a chair. "Cletus Bradberry's the name. But we must be talkin' about someone else. The Knettly family I know has been gone over forty years. Let's see James, Jim died in … '72, and his wife died at least 10 years before that. They didn't have any children, so no one's been on that place except to farm the land in over 40 years. They left the land in trust."

River's spine ran with chills. She couldn't find the words to speak. She met Thad's eyes, which were steady and calm.

"Was there ever a Tom Smith, the patriarch of a family up in that area? His wife's name was Mrytle and his son was Michael. Or maybe we're talking about another family?" Thad interjected.

"No sir. Like I say, Jim owned almost all the land from about a mile south of the interstate, all along the west side of 29 to the river. He even owned the bottomlands. Jim Knettly was the head of that family. He died in a tractor accident right on 29 in the winter of '72." Cletus shook his head. "Tragic."

"But I know I spent a night with a Smith family up there. Michael was big and tall, well over six feet. Tom wore a hat and had such rosy cheeks and Mrytle was... so kind." River said. "There must be another family we are talking about."

"They sound like nice folks, but I don't know who that'd be. James Knettly rolled his tractor down an embankment further up on 29 and he was crushed under it. They didn't find him till late afternoon. He laid there almost all day." Cletus sat for a moment. "All the good ones are gone, may they rest in peace."

"There's pictures a the Knettly's in the library. Stop by and ask for Millie, an old picture of them is on the conference room wall." Cletus tipped his hat as their waitress returned.

"What'll ya have?" The waitress sat down their drinks and took out her pad. Thad ordered and looked at River, who was white and pale.

"Honey?" Thad asked.

"I can't eat." River said, composing herself. "I'll just have a cup of warm tea, if you don't mind." She slid her iced tea away.

"Sure." The waitress turned and left the table.

River didn't hear the noise in the room any longer. "I don't know if I want to look at the Knettly's picture. What good will that do? Maybe the librarian will know where the Smith's live. What's happening to me? Was I knocked out? What about Sugar? Did you hear him talk about where James Knettly died?"

"I don't know what to think, honey. But I think we need to look at the picture, or you will always wonder." Thad was right.

Within an hour, they were at the library with Millie, who led them back to the empty conference room and flipped on the light. River's eyes were drawn immediately to the picture.

"That's not Tom, or Mrytle." She said. Thad stood behind her, and they looked at the couple in the picture together. "Remember how you felt when you couldn't figure out who or what you were looking at across the dam last December?" She asked him.

"Yep." Thad had seen the most beautiful, sparkling woman, who spoke to him with reassurance and love. For days after, he couldn't reconcile his senses with his mind. "I know how you feel."

"What do you mean?" Millie the Librarian asked.

"Two weeks ago, Tom Smith and his family took me in and kept me safe up at the Knettly house. I know I have the right house. Have you ever heard of Tom, Mrytle and Michael Smith? They entertained me. During that ice storm when my car went down an embankment, they got me out and kept me safe. I'd swear to it." River said, her eyes never moving off the Knettly's picture.

"I haven't heard of them. Let me check the county census for you. But you know what they say, the best hosts come for those in need" Millie answered. "I'll leave you to look around."

As they rode home, there were bouts of silence as River tried to process the day. While there were many Smiths in the county, there was no Tom or Thomas Smith married to a Myrtle. And there simply was no Michael Smith.

River finally broke the silence. "Thad... Am I crazy? How? Why?" River asked the questions that the faithful will sometimes ask, all the while knowing some questions are destined to remain unanswered. And so, they drove on.

"Come on Harry." Alvin stepped out into the December sunshine. "Time fer clearin'." He drove the 4 wheeler up to the machine shed that was in the woods off of Forest Drive behind the Craytons.

The doors were swung wide open. Wolfman ran out to greet Harry along with Duke. The three big dogs romped off into the woods leaving their occupied, and unconcerned owners to the snow plow and the tractor.

"The thing is man, you don't want to scrape all the rock off the road or we'll have a mess in April." Tim handed Dock a wrench to tighten a bolt on the side of the scoop.

"Yeah, but we gotta get the roads in better shape by tonight. It's too damn slick to be pullin' a bunch of carolers through the woods up here on Forest by the Daniels place. Let alone down the hills by the cliffs to Mimosa's Bounty.

"Hey fellas" Alvin stepped up. Alvin used to scrape the roads at Mimosa Lake, but Tim and Dock had taken it over after there were too many complaints of uneven roads.

"Whatta you doin' here? I thought you were gettin' the stuff ready for tonight." Dock asked as he reached for the larger wrench.

"All done with that. I wanted ta lil' time outta th' house. Peggy's doin' 'er nails. I done my last set a toenails cuz she cain't reach 'em." Alvin pulled his stocking cap down further over his white hair. He scowled at the thought.

"Gotcha man." Tim laughed a hollow laugh.

"Women." Dock concurred. "Alright boys, let's take 'er out for a cruise." With that he started the engine. "Ahhhh...purrs like a kitten." Dock took a puff on his cigar and backed 'er out of the shed.

By the time the sun set, cars filled the new Canopy parking lot and the road around it. More cars were traveling down the road by the cliffs to the Mimosa's Bounty offices and barns.

The younger men were all at their stations. Taylor Ivery, Jacob Latcher, Malkirk Mendez and Joos Jehan were driving the long caravan of carolers. Pastor Jack Daniels was in charge this year, along with Georgia Lemonn, who let's face it, never really gives up control of anything to anyone.

Each wagon had a leader and flashlights. Songsheets were plentiful. What had begun only a few years ago as a last minute idea with one wagon, was growing every year.

This left a dilemma, who to carol to? But it was quickly solved by expanding the caravan's journey to include Mimosa Lake Road.

Trixie Stokes Crayton sat next to River, their arms interlocked. Duke lay at Dock's feet next to Trixie and Sugar was on the other side of Thad between Sammi Clintston and Bunny Wright.

The roar of voices were silenced by Georgia on loudspeaker. Her voice rang out in the cold, clear air, barking directions and warnings about remaining seated. The caravan chugged up the hill.

Joos hit the brakes to remain a safe distance behind Taylor's wagon. He immediately noticed the brakes were soft, so he steadied the tractor down the small hill as best he could. When he tried the brakes again, they caught right away.

The carolers sang into the night, rounding Fern Drive in front of the Potts house, where Herbert's silhouette in his chair shown through the front porch windows. He didn't seem to budge as each wagon slowed, singing loudly up to him.

Extra time was spent at Todd Rolfes place. Since he'd lost his partner LL two years ago, Todd had experienced one illness after another. Unlike Herbert, Todd came to the front door in his warm robe and pajamas, waving and clapping in thanks.

"You'll be out here with us next year!" River called to him. She loved her neighbor, he was a kind man. She wished he would find someone, another partner. Todd was the type of person who was better off living with someone. Since he'd retired as the Forest Corners Postmaster General last year, she saw him outside less and less. River made a mental note, 'Call him tomorrow!'

And so on they went: singing, laughing and joking with each other under the December stars. Alvin's hot chocolate, Christmas cookies, cakes and other goodies awaited them at the Canopy. It was long after midnight when Taylor Ivery loaded the last group of carolers whose cars were down at Mimosa's Bounty onto the wagon to transport.

Rayme, Taylor's fiancé rode behind him on the last tractor that needed to be returned to the barn. Down the road cut into the steep cliffs in the moonlight. The moonlit snow sparkled against the dark, flowing Dogwood River.

Taylor tapped the brakes to slow the speed, but nothing happened. He lifted up and tapped again. The tractor was rolling faster than it should be to meet the upcoming curve.

"Hold on." He yelled to Rayme and the few people in the wagon behind. He downshifted and the motor revved, slowing the tractor enough to meet the curve.

"God, help us here." He said aloud, as he hit the brake again. This time it caught. He slowed even more as they rounded the curve. There was one more curve before the road leveled out.

"Hang on and pray, everyone." He called back to them. Rayme held on tight.

"Can you stop it and let them all jump off, Tay?" She yelled in his ear.

"I can't get it to stop, only slow down. I'm trying to get it into first." He wanted to get to level ground before he risked taking it out of gear.

Then, a brightness, flickering in the field beyond the barn caught his eye. In that short second he knew, all would be OK. He wasn't afraid, he just worked to keep it steady.

"We're alright." He called back. "Hang on, Ray-ray." He called back to Rayme. He took it out of gear just before the last curve and popped it into first, as the tractor kept rolling.

The engine ground down as they rounded the curve at a crawl. Then slowly, they descended down to the flat land.

When Taylor stopped the tractor near the side barn at Mimosa's Bounty, you could hear a pin drop. Then the praises began.

"Good job, Tay."

"Our prayers were answered."

"You saved us, Taylor."

"God helped us."

"Thank God you knew what to do, Taylor."

But Taylor knew, he had nothing to do with it. "There are these angels, you know." He later told Rayme.

She nodded in belief.

From the Angel's Hand
-6-

Herbert Potts sat alone in his TV room, eating his soup. That young girl, Mallie Jehan had brought it to him and left it on his step.

He'd seen her come up the driveway, with that little kid walking behind her as she brought the crock of soup to his door. He wasn't about to let some snot-nosed brat into the house to mess the place up.

She'd knocked and rang the doorbell. Once she met his eyes, but she'd had no reaction, so he knew she hadn't seen him behind the curtains.

"Come on, Emmanuel. Let's leave the soup for Mr. Potts. I know he'll find it." She offered her hand to the young boy who ran toward her as she walked down the steps. The walked back to their car together.

Once they were safely gone. Herbert stepped out and got the warm soup. It was wrapped in towels and tied with some string.

> *Mr. Potts,*
>
> *We had too much soup and thought you would like some. It's potato, ham and cheese, my mother-in-law's recipe. Hope you like it.*
>
> *Mallie Jehan.*

He wondered what she wanted. No one ever did a favor for someone without wanting something. She'd done this before a couple of times last winter.

He'd never said anything to her about it. He just left the empty crock on his front porch and he'd find it gone in a few days.

The soup tasted good, better than the canned stuff he was used to eating. Alvin had started cooking breakfast again at the Canopy, but he hadn't gone up there yet.

Part of him couldn't face them. He knew the way they talked about people. They probably had a good laugh over him. And he didn't need to be with those kinds of sinners.

Herbert was left to his own devices and that's how he liked it.

Next week he would go see Randi Kepter up at the state prison. He never knew what kind of greeting he'd get. One time she might actually talk to him, the next she'd refuse to see him. But God had sanctioned their union – through good and bad.

Now, they were walking through the desert together. The only problem was, Herbert felt more alone than he ever had in his life.

His heart began to ache at the prospect of another day alone and it didn't seem to stop. He watched Jeopardy as the pain in his chest sharpened. He took some short breaths to make it go away, but it moved down his arm.

Herbert is as short-sighted as his shadow at noon. But even in his blind righteousness, he is loved.

She stood in the corner of the room and watched him turn an ashen-white. It was all too familiar. She didn't know what would happen. She was not the determiner of life and death. She serves.

The phone rang. Herbert picked it up and dropped it on the floor. "Herbert, 't's Alvin. You 'lright?" Alvin Owens asked.

No answer. Herbert wanted to answer, but he couldn't get it out.

"Herbert? Herbert?" Herbert listened to his neighbor, hoping he'd figure it out. Alvin wasn't known for his brains.

"Hun.. I cain't get 'n 'nswer. Herbert, 'm comin' 'ver." He must have handed the phone to Peggy then because she came on.

"Herbert, Alvin's getting on the 4-wheeler and driving down. Please open the door for him if you can. Alvin! Take the key Selma gave us last year!" She called to her husband.

Herbert lay on the floor, the music of Jeopardy swimming through his head.

She stood with him, ready to take him if needed. But he remained, writhing in pain. She had seen humans in such circumstances before, and it always hurt.

There was a pounding at the door. "Herbert! Herbert! 'Comin' in." The key jiggled in the lock of the mudroom door and Alvin Owens stepped in. "Herbert!"

Herbert managed a groan. Alvin moved quickly for a man of his size. "Herbert! I'll call 'he ambulance." He grabbed his cell phone from his pocket. "911!"

Herbert could hear Peggy calling to Alvin on his phone that lay on the carpet.

Alvin picked it up. "Think he's havin' a heart attack. Get on 'ver here." He hung it up. "Yep, 'M here." He answered the operator. "Yep, that's right. 'K."

Alvin hung up and called Lucinda Peroze. "Lucinda, think Herbert's havin' a heart attack."

"I'll be right there." Lucinda hung up the phone. "Alvin says Herbert is down. I'm going to try to help." She left Samantha and Harris to finish their dinner.

By the time the ambulance arrived, Peggy and Alvin were assisting Lucinda who was on the phone with Darla, at the ambulance shed.

Herbert was covered and laying ready for the stretcher. He hated the idea of a Mexican working on him, but Lucinda Peroze had saved his life.

He'd been given another chance. Would he take it?

All any angel can do is pray. And prayer – is mighty.

They hadn't spoken much about it since the afternoon they had come home. River had been lost in her work all day. She had been commissioned by the Nature Conservatory in Minneapolis to paint six, 72-inch panels. Eagles were the central figures, but other elements of nature were to be depicted.

Hung along the walls of the studio were drawings of plants and animals, along with the six backgrounds for the panels. It was the largest job she'd ever had.

Around 2:30, she stopped to get a coffee refill and snack on a nectarine. The birds at the feeders were taking a rest before the big evening rush.

She loved her work, partially because she could take time to smell the roses. During the past week, she had contemplated on the Smiths quite often.

The thought occurred to her that she'd just passed out from the accident. After all, the dent in her front fender was real – to the tune of $637.18. She shook her head at the thought.

River wished for Frances Sullivan. At times like these, she could call her friend and invite her for tea and a chat. The world always seemed clearer after those chats.

The initial shock and numbness of death can cushion us from the reality of separation. River decided it was in the little moments, like this, that the pain of death was absorbed. Like small doses of sour-tasting medicine, just enough to reconcile and heal the soul - a spoonful at a time.

"I miss you, Frances. But I know you are with God." River spoke aloud to the coffee pot. And she knew, from the inside out, that Frances was happy.

River couldn't talk to Thad about this, and she didn't know why. He'd gone with her, he hadn't judged her. But she would've judged him if the roles were reversed. You disappear overnight, come back with a story about some wonderful, old-fashioned souls who took you in and now they are nowhere to be found.

"Too weird." River looked down at Sugar. "But you were there, unless it was a dream. And if it was, where were you?" Her mind went around in circles again. It was time to go back to work. She knew she had to put this mystery down, put it to rest for now. The day might come when she would have the answers, but for now, it wasn't going to be solved.

"Cobalt blue for the wash on this one." She spoke aloud, and Sugar raised her head for a moment. "You're not worried about it, are you Sugar?"

Sugar gave her the look of comfort that can only come from a dog's eyes. And River returned to her canvas.

W Wright hadn't thought a thing about his conversation with the pretty lady by the river. At 12 years old, he was still faithful and fearless.

Secretly, his mother prayed he'd keep his open-eyed wonder and acceptance of goodness into his manhood. But she realized that adolescence would somehow take its toll.

Missy Wright had managed the Raptor Society alone since Frances died. It was a larger job than she anticipated. Originally she'd been hired to write the grants for the foundation.

Missy was a talented grant writer. Not only was Scout Point Island donated to the Raptor Society, but now, they had almost enough funds to begin to build the Visitor Center and main offices for the Raptor Society. Today, she was going with Harris Clintston to meet with a contractor.

She took a last look in the mirror and adjusted the belt on her black dress before grabbing her coat. Harris was in the driveway.

'Wow! I guess we'll knock 'em dead today." Harris smiled. Harris was her neighbor and her friend. He'd advocated for the sizable raises that Missy had gotten during the past couple of years.

"Thanks. Sometimes I look at myself and wonder what would Carl think." Missy put her purse on the floorboard of the Escalade. She was referring to her deceased husband and the love of her life.

72

"He'd be proud of you, Miss. So proud." Harris patted her shoulder and pulled away. "Lucinda loaned me the Escalade, she thought it was too risky to be zipping around in the Lexus with the roads."

"Might make a better impression since we are asking for assistance." Missy added as they drove along. "Have you met this one?"

"Nope. Thad says he's good. If you want a road that's gonna last and the parking lot and grounds, solid, apparently Dale Overton is the one to call. Do you know him?" Harris asked.

"We've only spoken on the phone. He seems nice." Missy looked out the window as they zoomed along into Dogwood Bend.

Dale Overton stood up to greet them as they followed the hostess through the Limp Noodle to the back room. He put out his hand to Harris, who shook it firmly. Then offered it to Missy.

"So nice to meet you Mrs. Wright. I'd know you anywhere." Dale smiled. He had the long, lean look of honesty that Missy recognized, and liked.

They sat down to discuss business over lunch. Dale had acquired maps of Scout Point Island and already had a proposal for the road and facility.

"Mind now, this is just a rough idea. You won't hold me to it until I have a chance to see if everything checks out." He smiled at Missy, then met Harris with a firm, reassured, look.

"Of course. We appreciate you giving this as much thought as you have." Harris replied.

"Mr. Overton," She asked.

"Please, call me Dale. I wouldn't have it any other way." He interrupted her and threw off her train of thought.

It was hard to think with Dale Overton around. There was something about him... "Dale, can you supply me a list of your previous projects so I can pass it along to the Board? I need to see projects that were similar. It would be helpful." Missy asked.

"Anything I can do, Mrs. Wright." He answered with a smile as he took out his smartphone to make a note.

"And you can call me Missy. My husband, is deceased." She answered him as her phone began ringing. "Excuse me."

Missy got up and went to the lobby. It was the high school. Her heart always leapt when it was one of the kids. "Hello, this is Missy Wright." She answered.

"Mrs. Wright, this is Stacey Viddens." The Forest Corners School Nurse identified herself.

"Hi Stacey, what's going on?" Missy asked.

"Amelia is having some pretty bad cramping and bleeding. Mrs. Hullings found her in the bathroom doubled up on the floor of a stall. She brought her to me. Amelia feels that she needs to stay for her exam next hour, but Missy, I think she should be at home with her feet up."

"I don't have my car. I'm in Dogwood Bend in a meeting, but tell Amelia I'll be there in a half hour to drive her car home." Missy took a breath of relief. "Stacey, thanks. I'm sure we can find a way for her to make up her test. Can I talk to her for just a second?"

"Sure." Stacey handed the phone to Amelia.

"Just rest till I get there. Don't worry about your test, it'll be O.K. honey." Missy told her daughter.

"Mom, I lose points for taking it after today." Amelia's voice was weak.

"We'll work it out with Mr. Briggs." She reassured her daughter. "I'll be there soon."

Back at the table, Harris Clintston was getting the third degree.

"Please don't take me wrong. She seems like a wonderful lady." Dale Overton took a sip of his Pepsi.

"Yes she is. Inside and out." Harris commented as Missy returned to the table.

"I'm sorry, I have to go. Harris, will you drop me by the high school? Amelia is under the weather." Missy gathered up her belongings and reached her hand across the table. "Mr.... Dale. I hope we meet again very soon. I'm so sorry."

"Missy... he kept ahold of her hand longer than necessary, which captured her attention. "May I call you sometime soon to discuss a couple of things?"

"Sure..." Missy gave Harris a questioning look. Then she turned her attention back to Dale. "Of course. I'll look forward to it." She said as he dropped her hand.

Harris Clintston will swear to all who will listen that he does not like the spread of gossip. He believes it is unproductive, incorrect and often unkind. However, the minute Lucinda walked in the door that night, she could tell something was going on.

"You look like the cat who swallowed the canary, my love." She said as she kissed him hello.

That's all it took for Harris to sing like a bird.

Herbert Potts was resting comfortably that evening, surrounded by three of his children. Of course, Selma, his former wife had been called in Washington state. Selma was at Anna's, Herbert's estranged daughter.

"I don't want anybody else knowin!" Herbert hissed at his youngest son Fred.

"Dad, you had a heart attack. It's not a national secret." Fred, a man much like Herbert, replied. Fred regretted having to take the time out to get here. But there was the obligation.

Herbert sat with his dinner untouched. Later, alone in his room, he looked out the window into the dark winter sky. The lights in the hallway shone into his room and he could hear the nurses chattering.

But the dark sky drew him. Only then did he, almost unknowingly, let it slip out: "Why do I have to stay here? Why couldn't I just go on?"

The little boathouse had nothing but boxes and bedsprings in it. Moving day was here for the Jehans. Mallie and Victoria had spent a day cleaning the new house while 'Grandpa-pa Elmont' had watched Emmanuel.

Joos got a stack of sturdy boxes to put together from his employer. So all the UPS boxes were labeled and filled by moving day.

Jake brought the tractor with the flatbed attached. It was filled with friends and neighbors. Malkirk, Pastor Jack and several members of the Tree of Life Methodist Church, along with Taylor Ivery, Harris and Thad.

They'd have the Jehans moved in no time. Which was good, because Emmanuel Jehan's second birthday was tomorrow. Everyone was in a celebratory mood!

76

Victoria and Juliet Roach were keeping Emmanuel up at the Smythes' until the move was over.

They lifted and loaded. There were the usual jokes about how much stuff could anyone fit in the small boathouse. At the Canopy, Alvin and Elmont were making lunch for everyone.

Mallie, Felicia, EmmyB and Rayme were at the new house, directing the movers as they entered with the furniture and boxes.

Soon, Frances' former home was filled with laughter and the echos of voices asking: "Where do you want this?"

Even the December sun decided to show up for moving day. And it lit the way to a new home and a new beginning for the Jehan family.

That night, they lay in bed exhausted and holding their breath, because Emmanuel was sleeping in the next room for the first time in his life.

"It's like a dream come true." Mallie said as she rested in her husband's shoulder. "Except I never could have dreamed this."

"Me neither." Joos was falling asleep. "Mallie," He began. "For this new place to live and grow."

"For our friends - who are our family." Mallie continued their nightly ritual.

"For the boathouse, and Elmont and Victoria who didn't leave us out in the cold two years ago." He added.

"For Emmanuel, who is sleeping." Mallie said her mother's prayer.

"To you our God, we are so humbled." He took Mallie's hand.

"Guide us so we can share your blessings…" Mallie yawned. "Lord, forgive me, like the disciples, I'm so tired."

"Maybe he understands, just this once." Joos answered with closed eyes.

Their room was lit with a soft glow from the reflection of light on the lake. She stood at the foot of their bed, watching them rest as she so many times in the little boathouse. Peace was once again living at this place.

"I don't know why we didn't think of it before." Elmont said as he petted his cherished collie, Ravioli who was laying at his feet under the kitchen table.

"Well, I didn't know what you'd want to do with it. No one's ever lived in it until Mallie and Joos." Victoria sipped her tea.

"Victoria, maybe this is how we are to have children. Did you think of this?" Elmont's French-Canadian accent was heavy with emotion. "It is a fabulous idea my love. Do you have Jake's number?"

Victoria walked down the hall from the kitchen and into her office. She dug around for the number at Mimosa's Bounty.

"Here it is. They'll be at work by now." She handed Elmont the number.

"So early? After such a big day of moving yesterday?" He asked.

"Chef, they're young. You forget." She sat back down and wiggled her foot firmly in her house shoe, feeling glad to be her age and not a twentysomething.

"Yes, yes... you are so right. All that energy. Remember Montreal?" His face fell at the thought. "I hated it."

"That you did." She agreed.

"Mimosa's Bounty" Emmabella picked up the phone at the office. It was a Sunday morning, but the farm never stopped, no matter the day, even the Lord's day.

"Emmybella, so glad I could reach you." Chef Elmont began. "Victoria and I have been talking. You know how empty our little boathouse has now become since Mallie and Joos and the baby have moved?"

"Yes, I guess it does look kinda empty over there, Chef Elmont. You want us to keep an eye on it for you? We're right down here." Emmabella offered.

"Well, no..no.. Victoria and I would like you and Jake to consider moving into it. It probably is not as nice as your apartment in town, but we could work out a suitable rent. And it is close to the farm." Elmont tried to entice her.

"Yes! Yes!" Emmabella uncharacteristically screamed into the phone. "Oh Chef! Do you mean it? We would love it!"

Well… well… let me see if I have any hearing left!" Elmont laughed at her joy.

Even Victoria, who was known for her Canadian reserve, was smiling.

"This is wonderful news! We didn't know if you would like such a small place." Elmont laughed.

"Oh Chef! It's what we've been dreaming of. But, how much rent?" Emmy regained her composure.

"How much do you pay now?" Elmont asked.

"$400 for our apartment." Emmy told him.

"Then we shall say $200 plus the utilities." Elmont looked at Victoria, who nodded in agreement.

"You can't be serious?" Emmabella couldn't believe it.

"Child, it helps us to have responsible people there at the little boathouse. I hope you will find it to be a nice home. Can you bring Jake by later and we will sign the papers?" Elmont asked.

"He'll be out of the fields by 2:00, we'll be there at 2:15. And thank you so much." Emmabella's voice was deep with appreciation.

Elmont hung up the phone. "Victoria, what a wonderful day this has become!" Elmont smiled in that special way that warmed his wife's heart.

"Merry Christmas." She raised her teacup to him as Ravioli thumped her tail on the kitchen floor.

On a Wing and Paws
-7-

December 21st is a day of juxtaposition. On one hand it is the beginning of winter, the shortest day of the year at Mimosa Lake. Then again, it's only four days away from Christmas.

While Herbert Potts was convalescing at home, the long, cold days were on his mind. The house was quiet and dark and he liked it that way. At least the golf carts were safely stored away and not racing up and down Fern Drive kicking up dust everywhere. There was a silence as winter approached.

But in most houses around the lake, there were great preparations going on. Company was coming and no place was this more evident than at the Crayton household. Because a couple of Mimosa Lake's favorite visitors were on their way up from Tennessee: Beauregard and Mima Johnston, Trixie Crayton's parents.

Trixie had carefully placed the cypress Nativity set her father carved for them for their first married Christmas, in the bay window. She'd come home from work at Loli's by 3:30, half expecting Daddy's red truck to be in the driveway. But not yet.

As usual the dogs, Duke and Princess ran to greet her. Dock was in the back shed digging around. She had just enough time to check her crockpot and get a shower before he'd come inside.

"Hi Honey…" She yelled up to her husband. Trixie was filled with the Christmas spirit every time she came home to him. And today was no different.

He came out to the fence by the back gate, his cigar, a part of his silhouette, against the cool pinks and purples of the late afternoon sky.

"Be down soon, Honey. Take the little one inside, will ya?" He waved.

She waved in response. "Come on Princess, Daddy forgot your sweater again." She picked up the little shiatsu and walked up the steps. As if on cue, Duke turned and walked up into the back yard, returning to his master.

The house smelled wonderful, her roast was coming along. She'd pop a few carrots and potatoes alongside, then boil some extras. Daddy and Dock loved her mashed potatoes.

The fresh apple cobbler she made last night already had a piece out of it. She couldn't fault her husband, but she knew come January, the baking had to go. He was already complaining about his jeans being a little tight.

And oh, the tree! It was lit in the living room and the whole house smelled of fresh pine. They would plant it down by the other ones near the corner woods in the spring.

Trixie had just stepped out of the shower when the phone rang. She got it just in time.

"Hi Trixie, it's Mallie Jehan." Mallie said.

"Merry Christmas! How's the house?" Trixie asked.

"A blessing, a real blessing. I never knew how fast Emmanuel could run, and how far." Mallie laughed. "Thanks for asking, Trixie, I need some help."

"What is it?" Trixie asked.

"I've set up meals for Herbert Potts every day through January. But Todd got the flu yesterday and he can't get anything to Herbert tomorrow. Could you take him a plate?" Mallie asked.

82

"Oh Mallie, of course. We're having roast tonight, my folks are coming. Mama and I will make him up a feast." Trixie replied, then asked. "Who has tonight?"

"I can get something over to him later, as soon as Joos comes home to watch the baby. I'll get something together." Mallie answered.

"Nonsense. I have a bunch of food cooked here. Dock can run him over a plate for supper. We have so much stuff here." Trixie offered.

"Oh... that would be great. Want me to take tomorrow back then?" Mallie asked.

"Nope. We'll make sure he's good for the next couple of days. Is he going to the Canopy on Christmas Day?" Trixie asked.

"No... I mean I don't talk to him much. He doesn't feel well." Mallie didn't need to explain.

"Yeah...Well, thanks for thinking of us. We can help, just let me know. Merry Christmas, see you Christmas Day." Trixie signed off.

"Thanks again, Trixie." Mallie hung up. Two years ago they needed so much help. Now, she was thankful she could give back. A crash in the living room took her thoughts from her. "Mannie! Mommy is coming... what am I gonna find?"

"Noooo....." Her once-loving, perfect little baby yelled back. He's two now, that's for sure.

River had gotten the last of the house ready for her parents coming. They'd be here tomorrow. Thad was working late and was staying in town, which is why when the headlights flashed in her driveway, she didn't know who to expect.

Sugar barked, jumping at the door and wagging her tail. She must know whoever it is, River surmised. So she opened the door and walked out on the front patio to greet them.

Rounding the corner to the driveway she was stopped dead in her tracks. Sugar ran on to meet them as they climbed out of the red pickup.

"We thought we'd never find you. Sorry we came by this late, just on our way back home and had a Christmas present for you." Myrtle Smith climbed out of the pick-up with the help of her son Michael.

"Is it really you?" River couldn't believe her eyes as Sugar jumped at the back of the pick-up.

"Course it is." Tom Smith stomped his boots on the frozen gravel of the driveway.

River greeted them with open arms. "Come in, Come in." She motioned toward the front of the house. "Sugar, come here."

"Now, she comes by that honestly. Your Christmas present's back there." Tom nodded to Michael, who went around the back of the old pickup. "O.K."

Michael took down a young white dog from the back of the truck. River looked in disbelief as the dog came running towards her with Sugar.

"Rue? She looks exactly like Rue." She looked from one of them to the next. "Where did you find her? Is it a her? How on earth?"

"It's not how on earth, she's heaven-sent to you. We just delivered her." Myrtle said with a warm smile.

"Come here girl. Come here angel." River called the young white husky and she ran to River, jumping up on her.

"We know you had Sugar and all, but this one's special." Tom said.

84

"Very special." Michael added.

"Well, come on inside and let me get you something to eat and drink." River led the way into the house.

"Awww, River, this is so pretty with your Christmas tree and all the lights. What a beautiful spot." Myrtle commented as they rounded the corner and looked into the earth home through the windows that lined the front of the house.

"It's pretty fancy for our tastes." Michael laughed.

River got out an array of Christmas cookies, drinks, cheese and crackers. She offered chili and sandwiches, but the Smiths had eaten in Dogwood Bend.

"You must stay the night." She insisted.

"Naw, we're gonna go on home. It's only 7:00, just feels like midnight." Tom answered.

As they sat around the table eating and talking, the puppy examined the great room and River watched her closely.

"She's the spittin' image a ole' Rue up there on the wall." Michael observed. "We made a match."

"You certainly did." River replied. It was time to bring up the big question. "When Thad and I went to find the farm two weeks ago, you were nowhere to be found. But here you are, flesh and blood sitting at my dining room table. How can that be?"

They looked at each other and smiled, but it was Tom who answered. "Awww, River now you know we're right where we've always been. You come find us anytime you like."

River looked from one to the other. It made no sense. But she could feel their love. The search she and Thad had gone on didn't matter as much right then. "So, we'll keep in touch?"

"Child, of course we will." Mrytle grabbed her hand and River felt the warmth.

River to let it drop, for now. "What about staying the night? Seriously, Thad will be home tomorrow. It's so close to Christmas – and how am I going to explain another dog to him?" River laughed.

"You just tell him she's your Christmas angel." Myrtle answered. "If he's half the man I know he is, he'll understand."

"Yes, she is my Christmas angel. I'm going to name her Angel... What do you think?" River asked the Smiths.

"Sounds good, hope she lives up to it." Tom's reply brought a laugh from everyone. "Getting' late. Folks, got to get this show on the road."

"Oh! I've got a gift for you in the studio. Let me get it before you leave." River put on her jacket and they all went outside.

"So this is where you work, pretty little place." Mrytle looked around as River went to her canvas rack that stored all her work. She pulled it out. "Merry Christmas and thank you." She handed the painting to Mrytle.

"Oh my...it's lovely. Just the way it outta be. Tom, come look." She called out the door. Mrytle held up the painting in the light for them to see.

"It's the farm. River look at them eagles. Aren't they something? And there's the tractor and everything. That's mighty nice of you to paint the old place for us." Tom's eyes sparkled as he looked at the painting.

"It's how I remember it, the best of everything." River said. "I hope you'll enjoy it."

"Child, we love it. Thank you, honey." Myrtle gave her a hug and everyone walked out to the truck.

Michael was driving. "Better eyes than mine at night." Tom explained.

After their goodbyes, they piled in the truck and were off. River watched their taillights drive across the dam and make the right hand turn to head down toward Mimosa Lake Road.

The dogs were jumping and running around the yard at breakneck speed. Growling and playing.

River walked back to the studio and turned off all the lights. Then across the driveway they went. There was the kitchen to clean up, but first she'd call Thad. She was bursting with the news of the Smiths, and that other little angel.

"If that isn't the best cobbler, outside a your Mama's I've had in a month a Sundays, I don't know what is. Thank you Daughter." Beauregard Johnson leaned back in his chair with a deep sigh.

"Let's get the dishes." Mima stood up, but was interrupted by Trixie and the dogs.

"Mama, I'll get the kitchen." Trixie cleared the plates as if she was at Loli's, stacking them up her arm.

"What about supper for Herbert?" Dock asked.

"I've got it all warmed and ready in the oven. Why don't you and Daddy run it over to him?" Trixie took out the warmed plates, covered in foil and set them carefully in a basket. Then she tucked a towel around it and placed a layer of foil. On top, she placed the salad, whipped topping, butter and jello.

"I think he's gettin' the entire kitchen." Dock joked. "Come on Dad, let's go."

Beauregard got up. "A man gets no rest 'round here. Does he Dock?"

"Nope. Guess it makes for clean livin'." Dock took the basket and they left, Duke in tow trying hard not to sniff at the basket.

Mima treaded lightly in Trixie's kitchen. She knew how a woman felt about her kitchen. She had the same notion.

"Mama, how you and Daddy been feelin?" Trixie asked nonchalantly.

"We're O.K. The usual aches and pains. Daddy's a lot better than when you were down in October. He's gotten some medicine that actually works for the arthritis in his knees." Mima went on with news about Tennessee and what was going on at home.

As Trixie listened, she couldn't remember a time when she'd felt more at peace. Christmas was here.

The beds at Georgia's house on the hill, aka: Georgia's castle were filling up with children and grandchildren. Felicia had her own room, because she lived with her grandmother while she was attending her second year of college. But even Felicia was sharing her bed with her sister, Lauren, in from the east coast.

Georgia was in her element. She organized activities, bossed the daughters and daughter-in-law's around the kitchen and handed out what she perceived to be words of wisdom on child rearing.

Christmas Eve morning, Bellamy Whitfield, Georgia's main squeeze, came out from the city to be with the family. He attended Christmas services at the Oak Street Baptist Church in Forest Corners with Georgia, then left to spend Christmas Eve with his son in the city. They all would be out for Christmas afternoon at the Canopy.

As usual, Piers and Deborah Ivery arrived on the 23rd. This year grandson Taylor picked them up from the airport and deposited them safely at his AR's at Mimosa Lake.

88

River ran to greet them from the studio when she saw Taylor's truck coming down the driveway. There was nothing like seeing her parents.

After getting settled, they waited dinner on Thad, who managed to make it to River's just as they debated how much longer the spaghetti could stay warm and the bread wouldn't burn.

"Thadius!" Piers gave his son-in-law to be an open armed bear hug. "Still on the run after the almighty dollar?"

"Looks that way, more like after the almighty client. Wish some of 'em would get more of the Christmas spirit. How are you Piers?" Thad smiled warmly as he hugged him, then he stepped toward Deborah. "There she is!" He wrapped his arms around River's mother. He truly loved the thought of belonging to the Ivery clan, especially after last year when they had rebuilt the golf cart for River.

"So good to see you." Deborah gave Thad a big kiss and hug. "How's your Mom? I haven't talked to her since Thanksgiving, is she still coming?"

"Yep. She'll be here tomorrow." Thad's green eyes sparkled with joy. "So what do ya think of the newest edition to the family?" Thad petted Angel, who stood beside him waiting her turn.

"She's Rue reincarnated. It's uncanny." Deborah replied and then leaned into him. "River's being funny about her."

"It's a long story. But we're happy she's here, right honey?" Thad asked his bride-to-be.

"What? River called from the kitchen as she opened to top of the pot of sauce.

"Angel, we're glad she's here, no matter how she got here. Right?" Thad repeated.

"Made my Christmas!" River turned to the oven, to check the bread. "It's time, let's eat."

Deborah's heart was warmed. River finally seemed happy. She trusted again. Just over a year ago, Deborah had sent Piers back to Arizona. She was so afraid for River that she stayed with her through those dark days filled with accusations and depression.

Last Christmas had been a start, but this year, River had turned a corner. She was confident again. Her life was opened up and now, Angel. There were better days coming, and more times of celebration.

"Amen." She said aloud.

"What Mom?" River asked.

"Amen, to life." Deborah answered.

River smiled and nodded at her mom. "Amen."

Christmas Eve supper at the Smythes was as good as ever, but there was a moment when Frances came to mind.

"She must have carried the spirit of Christmas all year long." Joos Jehan said. "How could she even think to give strangers her house?"

"She was a wonderful, loving person. And somewhere, she's celebrating tonight." Victoria replied. "Don't you think so?"

"I know so." Juliet Roach lifted her glass. "A toast to Frances: we grieve her, we miss her, we rejoice that she was our neighbor and friend." Juliet lifted the glass.

"So many people pass by, all too quick. It took looking death in the face for me to appreciate life." Zigler Roach said, referring to his cancer scare in 2009.

"It must be the way we learn, my friend." Chef Elmont placed a baked apple onto a small plate and passed it down the table to

Mallie to cut up for Emmanuel. "When I was stranded on Scout Point Island so long ago, I knew my life must change. Why I could not come to such a realization in the living room in my chair by the fire, this, I do not know."

Everyone laughed, identifying with Chef's truth. The soft lights, the smell of pine, the lit fireplace and the tired two year old were all conducive to the Christmas spirit. Grace and happiness filled the rooms of the big, warm house. Outside, the cold December air, illuminated the bright waning moon.

He'd helped Dock and Alvin cut wood two days ago, that's probably what had made his back all the worse. Tim Cole lay in his bed on Christmas Eve, staring out the window.

Wolfman, his trustworthy hound lay snoring on the floor below. Wolfman's long legs stuck out into the room and his paws moved every so often, as if he was running in his dreams.

Tim waited for the dose of medicine to take effect and put him into a deep sleep. He knew this was no way to live. He rolled back slightly, just enough to see the long hanging above the bed.

"*God Bless this Union*". Teresa had hung it there when they moved in the house too many years ago to count. Now, she snored as she lay next to him, facing the other side of the room. They didn't sleep together when no one was in the house. Tim shook his head at the thought. There was a day when he and Teresa had hid the fact they were sleeping together, now they were hiding the fact that they weren't.

The kids were downstairs, out from the city. Tyler had breezed in about 9:00. Melanie and husband Bobby had come about 3:00. Melanie had tried to get her Dad alone to talk to him, but Tim didn't need to confide in his daughter, not about this stuff.

Tim Cole was going through the motions, without purpose and without hope. Hope. His thoughts stuck on the word and he painfully turned toward the window again. Teresa mumbled some comment in her sleep. He wondered how she did it. Even when she was unconscious, her tone was harsh and sarcastic.

His thoughts drifted back to the days of his short-lived affair with Kalista Riner. The sex was great, he hadn't felt like a man for years before – or since. But it was more. He'd felt like a man, liked for who he was. There had been good years with Teresa, but they were in high school. He was almost 60.

Like his father Josiah, he saw himself fading away. And with that thought sleep overtook him.

But as it is with all troubled souls, he was being carefully watched over. She stood near him and listened to him breathing. Filled with love and grace, she breathed upon him.

Tim Cole is one of the good ones. Too good to let go.

Sound the Trumpets!

-8-

Sound the trumpets! Christmas Day is here! The eagles were up at daybreak in search of food, scanning the Dogwood more these days than Mimosa Lake. The lake was freezing over in spots and the fish were at rest, making them easy targets on warmer days, but dead weight that sank deep when the air crackled with cold, like this Christmas morning did.

'River's eagle', stopped by to sit in the arching oak tree down by the dock above Rue's grave. It gave Deborah Ivery a thrill to sit in the living room and watch him. She enjoyed the peace, there wasn't much time to prepare for the day.

Last year, they'd had all been at Eddie and Mia's in town. Today, the family would join the Mimosa Lake neighbors in the to celebrate. It was the first Christmas the new Canopy was standing.

River walked sleepily out of her room and grabbed some coffee from the perking pot in the kitchen. "Merry Christmas, Mom." She kissed her mother and sat down beside her.

"I've been watching the eagle on your tree. He's beautiful and so big!" Deborah commented. "Merry Christmas." She kissed her daughter and held her close. "It's a good Christmas, this year."

"Yes, it is." River smiled, sipping her warm coffee. "Did you see the moon last night, almost full on Christmas Eve. It was like daylight.

"Mmmm... I was snoring right alongside your father." She laughed.

"I never snore, I breathe with gusto!" Piers Ivery rounded the corner by the dining room. "Merry Christmas Wife and Daughter! Where's that Sandberg fellow? Is he one of those who sleeps till noon?"

"No, he's up. He's on the phone with his mom, making sure she knows how to get here. She's been here three times, but he worries she'll take a wrong turn and get lost." River poured her dad a cup of coffee. "Merry Christmas, Dad." She held him tight and kissed his cheek.

"Well, Dock and his father-in-law need help at the Canopy moving those fryers before they get too hot. Harris just called me." Thad reported. "How long till breakfast, honey? Merry Christmas." He took his fiancé in his arms and kissed her gently. Touching his head to hers and looking into her blue eyes he smiled. "Again." He said, raising his eyebrows.

"Thadius, have they roped you in already?" River asked.

"Honey, it'll probably take 15 minutes." Thad turned to his soon to be in-laws. "Merry Christmas! Piers, wanna come?"

"If I could be any help. Mother?" He looked at Deborah who waved him on. She remained sunken into the couch, not wanting to move yet.

"Get your coat. River, I'll take the jeep." Thad walked toward the door with Sugar and Angel in tow. "O.K. you can come too." At this the dogs leapt in the air and ran to the door. Sugar relaying her pleasure in 'dog talk'.

The quiche was on the bake and the cinnamon rolls were on their last rise when River returned to the couch by her mom. Her mother brushed her long hair back with her fingers. "You seem happy together, is it all going alright?" She asked.

"It's going better than I thought it could. Mom, it's an adjustment to live with anyone. But sometimes, Thad stays in town. I used to like it more than I do now. Now I miss him when he's gone."

"Just so you're happy. It's a big step, you've lived as a single woman for so long. This will be a busy year, with the wedding, but it will be a good one. Finally, I'll be a mother of the bride." Deborah held up her coffee cup and clinked it to River's.

All around Mimosa Lake, Christmas was being rung in, from house to house. Keeping with traditions, the Clintston/Peroze household opened the gifts early Christmas morning. Samantha Clintston was the baby of the family at nine, so everyone slept in until a reasonable hour. Jake and Emmabella would stop by on their way to the Canopy later this morning after spending time with the Mayers, Emmy's parents.

Sammi had gotten the new IPad she'd asked for and the new backpack for dance. But it was the set of pastels, paint, canvas and papers that she'd been the most thrilled with when she unwrapped it.

"If you love to your art, Sam, better have the good stuff to work with." Her daddy had winked his twinkling blue eye at her. "Guess the old guy at the North Pole knows that."

"Dad..." Sammi smiled at him.

"Listen to your father, he's a wise man." Lucinda told her daughter in heavily-accented English.

"Si, Si, Mama." Sammi helped pick up the wrapping and then set the table for the three of them. She talked to Uncle Eduardo and Aunt Maria in Texas, then the family in Mexico before going to her room.

There it stood, her beautiful creation. Even her parents didn't know about it, only Bunny Wright. She'd give it to Mrs. Lemonn this afternoon and maybe, they would like it.

Samantha Clintston was a child with an old heart and wise soul. She'd already learned the true joy of Christmas was not in receiving but in giving.

She couldn't wait till this afternoon.

Christmas Eve service went like a dream at The Tree of Life Methodist Church, leaving the Pastor to enjoy his first Christmas with baby Grace, who had magically slept through the night. This gave them just the boost they needed to get through the day.

The Mendez family was packed into the Daniels house. Malkirk was home from the school and the city and Nakita's parents were in from California.

There was a great and spicy breakfast with all the dishes Barbara Mendez had made since the dawn of time – or so it seemed to Nakita.

Everyone compliment Jack on the his Christmas sermon again and after breakfast, before Malkirk went round the lake to Felicia's (Georgia's), the gifts were given, open and joyfully received.

Meanwhile, the colorful pepper dishes, black beans and rice with sausage and the burrito casseroles bubbled away in the kitchen. All would be carted up to the Canopy in a couple of hours. There was great Christmas cheer, but few could match surprise and hoopla of Trixie Crayton next door.

Last year, Dock had gone looking for a dog to fill the void that the death of Trixie's childhood dog had left so long ago. Well, he fell in love, not with one, but two strays that had bonded so closely together at the shelter that they had to be adopted together. Trixie was thrilled. Princess and Duke had changed the Crayton household – and the Craytons.

"I don't know 'bout these dang dogs runnin' the house. Back home, they'd be out in a pen." Beuaregard Johnson had to comment, but he'd been found sleeping with Princess on his lap. And Duke had followed him around like there was no tomorrow through the back woods yesterday.

How could Dock top last year? But early this morning when Trixie had opened her gift, she was thrilled. It was a large, solitary pink diamond on a gold chain.

"Oh, Dock! You are so good to me." Her brown eyes watered up and she kissed him in front of her folks, which slightly embarrassed him.

"Nothin' to it." He'd mumbled. Then he winked at Beauregard and Mima.

"Oh Dock, it's just beautiful. It's so big! Look Mama." She said as she put it on. Secretly, Trixie was glad she'd gotten him that new hunting stand. She'd debated the expense, but gone ahead.

After the gifts were opened and breakfast was done, Dock was getting ready to go up and help at the Canopy. "Can you all help me load truck?"

The Johnsons knew that was their cue. "We'll all help." Mima told her son-in-law.

"Awww...Mama you don't have to go out in the cold. I'll do it." Trixie went to get her coat. And everyone, walked over to the garage.

"Thing is, I'm gonna need a bigger garage. I'm thinkin' a buildin' another one just behind the shed up there." Dock pointed up the hill as he spoke to Beauregard, loudly so Trixie could hear.

"Oh Dock, we don't need any more garages, honey. We have so much stuff. We just need a good cleaning come spring." Trixie took Mima's arm and waited for him to open the garage door.

But the first door didn't open, instead the third door opened and inside the third bay, Dock stood smiling ear to ear. "Merry Christmas honey!"

Inside sat the most beautiful pink and white golf cart with silver trim. The top was fringed in pink and the headlights had eyelashes around them. The word 'Trixie' was spelled across the front hood in white with silver sparkles. The white seats were padded with pink pads and there was a pink pet carrier seat facing backwards on the back seat.

Trixie didn't know what to do. She simply broke down and cried.

"Awww Honey, I didn't do it for you... We have to keep up with River in her snazzy golf cart." Dock puffed on the cigar in his mouth, smiling ear to ear as his wife held him tight.

"I .... Don't .... Know.. what to ... say... It's beautiful." Trixie wiped her eyes, luckily her mascara was waterproof. Dock handed her a paper towel from the garage and she used it.

"I'm telling you honey, this man loves you!" Mima said as she walked around admiring the cart.

"He must. I wouldn't thinka turnin' your Mama loose on onea these things." Beauregard's comment made everyone laugh and lightened the mood.

"Take it for a spin!" Dock encouraged her.

"Oh no! It could get muddy." Trixie looked at the little heart that hung from the top of the rear view mirror.

"It'll clean up. Take your Mama down the road while we go up to the Canopy." Dock pulled the key from his pocket, it hung from a large, pink, furry di.

Trixie got in and started the cart.

"Look here, honey. I had 'em put a gas gauge in it so you can see how full it is. Just let me know when it needs fillin'. And there's the reverse – right there." Dock gave her a few instructions.

But within a few minutes, Trixie and Mima were down the driveway and had turned left toward the junction of Fern and Forest drives.

Mima saw the glee of her childhood within her for the first time since she'd left home after high school. *Thank God for Douglas Crayton.* She rejoiced with a Christmas prayer. *And Alleluia*

Jesus!

Georgia couldn't remember when the Canopy had been so packed. She didn't really have time to think about it anyway. Thad's design of the building had taken what they loved and made it better. Now, instead of the bar and patio being off in another room, there was one great room that two sets of double doors entered.

There was a glassed in patio and an outdoor patio that remained permanently covered with a bright tin roof that complimented the Canopy's reds and blues.

The line of windows facing Mimosa Lake had been doubled and still ran up the 18 and 28 foot ceilings. Now the kitchen was to the road side of the building, which made it easier for deliveries and the dining room looked down the hill to Mimosa Lake and the lower lawn and patio.

Some of the stone had been salvaged from the fire and was rebuilt into the large fireplace that was between the double doors and in front of the coat room. Large steps and a ramp circled it, leading guests into the great room and bar area.

But the 18 foot Christmas tree stood near the center peaks of the building and captured everyone's attention this Christmas Day. It was lit with new LED lights that changed colors. True, it was sparsely decorated, even though Beverlee's Bunch, the Mimosa Lake crafters had worked on decorations all fall. Time would fill in the large trees that would stand over future Christmas'.

The room was filled with joy and good cheer. Everyone was admiring Trixie Crayton's new golf cart and Dock was beaming with pride.

His wife, appropriately dressed in a winter white Christmas pink poinsettia sweater that showed off her new pink diamond and winter white satin pants with pink heels. Trixie was beaming. Her hair, was piled on top of her head and tied with a single ribbon and pink poinsettia. "He didn't do it to outdo yours, River." Trixie was explaining.

"Of course not, it's beautiful! And it's so...you!" River smiled and giggled.

"Onea these years, you're gonna have to build her the Taj Mahal in your backyard if you keep outdoin' yourself." Loli, Trixie's boss and surrogate mother jibed Dock as she took a drag off her cigarette. Loli came with the Craytons to all Mimosa Lake events, she was one of the family. And she always found herself in the kitchen with the men.

"Naw..." Dock quipped back. "I figure I'm good for a couple a years, then I can get back to toasters."

"You'll be toast then." Loli finished her cigarette. "Time to see if Alvin's gonna burn down this kitchen. Hate to leave you alone with this one, Tim."

100

"Yeah, thanks." Tim was overseeing the smoking hams and turkeys. He turned back to the smokers and took a sip of beer.

"You're quiet today." Zigler Roach patted Tim on the back. "Feeling poorly?"

"Naw, Man... it's a constant thing. You know." Tim answered. "Glad we're back up here celebrating though." Tim tried to be positive. The group stood enjoying the outside air.

"Yeah, it's great Dad." Tim's son-in-law took a sip of beer. "We could be alone. And times are rough enough, without being alone on Christmas Day."

Franklin Sheldon joined the group for some fresh air just as the topic had come up. He mouthed his pipe and took a puff. "Anybody seen Herbert?" He asked.

The general response was no.

"We ought to see 'bout him. Today of all days. He sits alone too much." Alvin wiped the sweat from his round brow. He'd stepped out for air.

The conversation, the bright sunshine and Christmas Day brought the men around to a plan. Alvin, Dock and Elmont would go get Herbert and try to talk him into comin' out. Loli took over the kitchen and the men left.

Beverlee Sheldon inspected the tree. It was lovely, just not really decorated. She'd found an old star at a thrift shop in town to top it, but it didn't really shine until night time. "I don't know, seems like we just ran out of time. We certainly have our work cut out for us." She told Todd Rolfes, who was a member of the Bunch.

"I found some patterns for woven ornaments that are just beautiful. Of course who will want to do ornaments in January?" Todd rolled his eyes.

"Bring 'em anyway!" Beverlee waved to Leah, Georgia's daughter who was in from the west coast. "Doesn't Leah look pretty?"

"She's a lovely woman." Todd offered as he watched Dock, Elmont and Alvin walk in the front doors. "Wonder where they've been?"

"Who knows, admiring Trixie's golf cart. He's prouder of it than she is." Beverlee laughed as she put her arm around her daughter (by choice), Ellenour. "Where's Nate?"

"Hi Todd, Out with Harris, Thad, Jake and Joos getting the wagon ready for hayrides.

"Guess the tractor's fixed." Beverlee offered.

"Yes, or there would be no rides." Lucinda stepped into their circle as she walked by.

Across the room Samantha Clintston was about to make her move and she was nervous. Mrs. Lemonn was walking with her granddaughter from the east coast, toward the patio area.

Sammi ran up behind them. "Mrs. Lemonn. Mrs. Lemonn?"

"Sammi, how are you? This is Lauren. Lauren, Samantha Clintston." Georgia's green eyes met Sammi's dark ones.

"Mrs. Lemonn. I need to show you something. Do you have time to look?"

"Sure." Georgia put her arm on Sammi's shoulder. The child seemed out of sorts. "Are you alright?"

"Yes, yes..." Sammi took her hand and led them to side meeting room off the hallway to the kitchen.

"This is all very secret." Georgia exclaimed to Lauren. "A mystery." She said when they saw Bunny Wright standing inside the room and a large cloth covering something on the table.

102

"If you don't like it, you don't have to keep it. It's my first." Sammi tried to explain. "I saw her out here and I wanted to make something. Mama and Daddy don't know about it."

"I'm sure it's very nice, child. Let's see." Georgia replied.

Samantha lifted the cloth off the figure who sat staring at them. Her champagne colored dress was made of silk with treated burlap overlaid as a coat. Her lace wings were almost in motion. Her blonde hair seemed to move, even though she sat still and her eyes were bright with light. Her small chin rested on one of her delicate fingers and her feet were in ballet shoes with ribbon laces up her legs that went under her long silky dress.

Georgia, rarely at a loss for words, was at a loss for words. They all just looked at her for a moment. "She's beautiful. And where did you get her?" Georgia asked, diverting her eyes toward Sammi for a moment.

"I made her. I saw her out my window. She was standing in our yard by the pine trees toward the dam. I told her I wanted to make her into a doll, so she could watch over the Canopy and everybody at Mimosa Lake. She said O.K." Sammi's eyes were wide with thought.

"So she's a person, who came to visit you?" Georgia asked. Then she remembered. "You know, I saw someone like her out my window one afternoon."

"She likes to visit here." Bunny Wright piped up matter-of-factly.

"Sammi, she's beautiful. You've done a wonderful job, child. I don't know why you don't want to tell Lucinda and Harris about her. They would be so proud of your hard work." Georgia encouraged her.

"No, Mrs. Lemonn, no. I want to give her to you, for the Canopy. I want her to stay here and watch over us." Sammi went to the beautiful figure she'd created and touched her lovingly, as if to say goodbye. "I want you to have her."

"Oh Samantha, what a gift! Are you sure?" Georgia asked again.

"Yes. I'm sure." Sammi answered.

"She's so pretty, Gram. You did great." Lauren complimented Sammi.

"Well let's show her to everyone." Georgia decided.

The fire crackled and the Canopy was warm, even downstairs, the rooms were warm. Activity, neighbors, chatter, fire and the Christmas Spirit set the building ablaze – in a good way.

As dinner was winding down, Georgia stood up at her table and tapped her glass. Madam President of the Mimosa Lake Organizing Board had an announcement.

"Everyone! Everyone! Just a few words." Georgia spoke and the room quieted down. She eyed Sammi and nodded. Sammi got up and left the dining area.

"Well, Merry Christmas!" Georgia greeted them. And the crowd returned a resounding holiday cheer. "Pastor Jack mentioned in his prayer how blessed we all are and I agree. We have our Canopy back, new and improved."

That was met with a great deal of cheer. Georgia let it die down as Sammi entered the room with the draped figure and came over to her.

"Right here, honey." Georgia pointed. "These days as we all watch the news, we can get rather discouraged at the state of affairs our world is in. Remembering that Jesus Christ was born on this day to save us and to encourage us, helps. But daily life

104

can sometimes tear away at the hope we have in Jesus." The crowd murmured in response. Georgia took a breath, held up her finger and took a sip of water.

"Yet, the hope we have in Jesus is all around. Right here at Mimosa Lake, I see neighbor helping neighbor again and hope being restored as young people come and bring new life to our shores. This afternoon, Samantha Clintston offered a gift to our community. I'd like you to see it and then she can tell you about it. Sammi?" Georgia nodded at Sammi. "Harris, Lucinda, "I gave her permission to stand on this chair." Georgia smiled.

"I made this for the Canopy. I hope you'll want it." Sammi bent over and took the figure out from under the cloth and held it up with Georgia's help.

The 'oooowwwwwwwww.....' from the crowd said it all.

"That's beautiful. She made that?" Beverlee whispered to Franklin who nodded with a smile.

Then applause broke out. Sammi blushed at the reaction. Georgia gave it a minute.

"I guess you've had my reaction! Sammi MADE this. I thought she'd bought her." Georgia turned to Sammi.

"I saw a lady like her in our yard by the pine trees. She's so pretty. I asked if her if I could make this for us and she said OK. I want her to stay at the Canopy." Sammi handed the angel to Georgia.

"Samantha, on behalf of the MOB, I accept your work of art. There's a special ledge at the peak of the great room. Dock, can she sit up there?" Georgia asked.

"You bet. If that's where you want her." Dock replied. "Sam, great work!" Everyone cheered in response.

Lucinda and Harris were bursting with pride when they were hit with the cold breeze that came in the side door of the dining room. Everyone turned to look and the room fell quiet.

A crumpled and gnarled hand held the door open as the clinking and clanking of a wheelchair rolled slowly through it. Tim Cole got up to help.

"I don't need help." The surly, all-to-familiar voice of Herbert Potts bit through the room like the cold air he'd brought with him.

"Just givin' you a hand, man." Tim didn't back down. Herbert rolled in and around the tables in the back with only a few welcomes being given.

Georgia took her opportunity. "Herbert, I'm so glad you could make it to our Christmas."

"I'm not here for you to feel sorry for me. I'm just fine at home. But they came," He nodded towards Dock and Alvin. "Pushin' on me to come over for the neighborhood."

"Well, let's get you a plate and a place." Georgia looked at Juliet Roach who was near the food and she got up and began working on a plate.

"I won't be here long, I know how most of you feel 'bout me and Randi." He looked around at all the eyes of judgement cast upon him. "Judge me if you like. But she's a good woman... you just... don't know..." He looked down and reached for his handkerchief in his pocket. "Judge me... all ya like..."

"It's Christmas Day, Herbert. Jesus doesn't want me to stand here and judge you. It's not my place to judge you, it's my place to forgive you and love you. And I do." River was standing across the room, her legs shaking under her and she didn't even know why. "And Herbert, I've forgiven Randi... somehow." She reached for Thad's hand and held it tight.

"I don't need your love and I don't need your forgiveness." Herbert looked up. "I don't need it from any of you... I'm fine..." He glared at River and then, his eyes began to blur. And then, in front of all his neighbors at Mimosa Lake and beyond...

106

Herbert Potts began to cry. And his crying led to sobs. And all could see the great pain this surly, broken man was in.

Juliet silently sat a warm plate of food in front of him and stood back as River walked to him.

"Herbert, I'm sorry for your hurt. I pray the Lord blesses you and eases your burden." And with that she bent down and kissed top of his head. Holding his sobbing shoulders.

Georgia stood behind her as River raised up and placed her hand on his shoulder. "Herbert, we are your neighbors, here to help you. God Bless you."

Pastor Jack stood over him and blessed him. "Lord forgive this man and heed the great pain he is in. As his brothers and sisters in

Christ, we pray for his joyful redemption."

"Amen" Many said in the crowd.

And one by one, they came. And one by one, they greeted him and gifted him with forgiveness.

And finally, Herbert ate his Christmas dinner. And it tasted like none he'd ever eaten before.

Into the night, the neighbors celebrated together. It had been a joyful, wonderful, Christmas filled with unexpected twists and turns.

Last year, River Ivery was given a golf cart for Christmas. It was a step – or a roll – in the right direction. This year, she'd been given the gift of freedom, by the grace of God's forgiveness.

She sat with Thad in silence, looking out at Mimosa from their bedroom. The dogs were sleeping on the floor, the cats were draped around, deep in their winter naps. A single candle was lit on River's prayer table by her chair on 'her side' of the room.

River and Thad reveled in the comfort of grace. Each thinking about the magnificence of the day. Jesus brought heaven to earth so long ago. He bound us together as one and gave us the tools we need to live our lives.

But just in case we're blinded, or stubborn, or just plain lose our way, there's always an angel or two around for good measure.

The Canopy Christmas tree was lit for all to see. Even sitting on the hill so far away from the shoreline, Mimosa Lake reflected its light on the cold, dark rippling water.

She stood alone, under her likeness above. And she was happy. As the lights around the lake twinkled off one by one, each in a deep peaceful silence that only a cold winter night can bring. All the lights were out now. The eagles, and the birds, the fox and even Mimosa Lake woodchuck were fast asleep.

But this was a time of rejoicing! Today, hearts were drawn together, love was practiced and people were beginning to see. The hope of heaven and earth was alive! She could hear praises being lifted in song from above.

Looking up, she ascended into the light. It was time to sing for joy!

THE END

A NOTE FROM THE AUTHOR

Dear Friends,

There was a change at Mimosa Lake this Christmas, a tipping point. I realized it within minutes of writing the last paragraph. All of my work is planned, sometimes months or even years in advance. I'm teased about it by many of my writer friends. No matter, it's what makes me comfortable. When I 'map out' a book, the true story lines begin.

But when I actually write the book, always, inevitably it takes on a life of its own. Characters decide they can't do what I intended, circumstances change. I'll go to bed exhausted and wake up with a new story line. I live where I'm writing. Writing Angels on High has been a wonderful trip home to Mimosa Lake after a year of absence.

So what changed? I did! And because of it, all the neighbors at Mimosa are speaking to me differently. Especially River and the Angel. The more I live my faith, the more the line between my 'truth' and God's intentions for me narrows.

The neighbors at Mimosa Lake don't question the presence of God...they count on God's presence. It sounds like a simple thing, but counting on – trusting God fully – is the key to taking our lives to the next step. With God, because of Jesus' birth and life, we can soar with the eagles and fly with the angels. Jesus came is the bridge to understanding between heaven and earth. Because of Christ, we are able to live on a higher plain. So will you come fly with me?

Keep an eye out for eagles.

OTHER BOOKS BY K. S. WUERTZ

THE MIMOSA LAKE SERIES

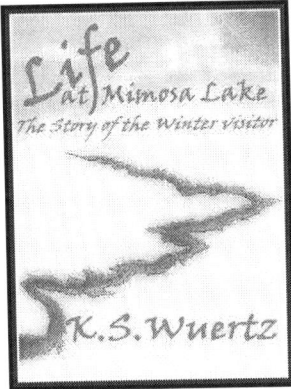

The Story of the Winter Visitor (Vol. 1)
The recession has left River Ivery and her Mimosa Lake neighbors feeling isolated and hopeless. River knows something must change. But how? God=s answer is the Winter Visitor. With loving presence, the Visitor offers renewal to the neighbors. But will they take it? Only the coming of spring will tell.

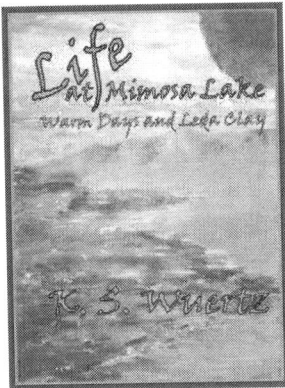

Warm Days and Leda Clay (Vol. 2)
Thanks to the eagles that wintered at Mimosa Lake, the neighbors are looking forward to spring. But are they just standing on Leda Clay? Join River and all her Mimosa Lake neighbors, as they rely on their faith to give them sure footing through an ever-changing landscape. With God's help, they just might learn that falling down a slippery slope can land you in unexpected blessings.

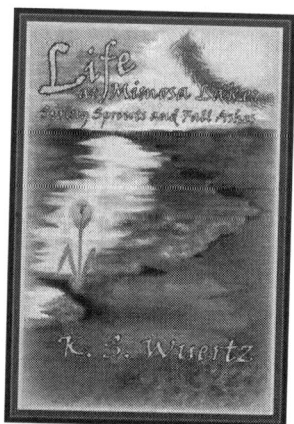

Spring Sprouts and Fall Ashes (Vol. 3)

The neighbors have come to expect the unexpected at Mimosa Lake - and to rely on the eagles to fly in with the promise of better days on their wingtips. Yes, the eagles are nesting on Scout Point Island, but where are those better days? Join River, Dock, Georgia, Herbert, Tim and all the neighbors, as they are tested in a firestorm of fear, grief, heat, lust and loss. But with God's help, and under the eagles' watchful eyes, the neighbors may discover that the strongest spring sprouts grow from fall's ashes.

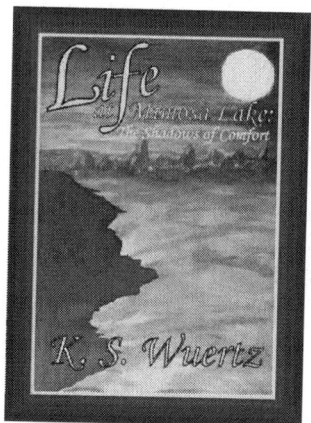

The Shadows of Comfort (Vol. 4)

Who would burn down the Canopy? The accusation of arson against River Ivery has catapulted her into a spiritual desert. Dock Crayton knows his wife Trixie, and River are innocent. But how can he prove it? Is there light amongst the shadows? Join the Mimosa Lake neighbors as they wait, search and walk through the sand and the shadows. Maybe comfort rests in the darkest of shadows. After all, all darkness rests against the light. Doesn't it?

114

THE MIMOSA LAKE
CRHISTMAS SERIES

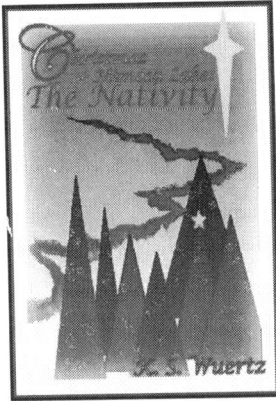

The Nativity (Vol. 1)

In December 2011, Mimosa Lake is cluttered with unfulfilled wishes, burned out buildings, strange people and tempers flaring. What a season! River, Dock, Georgia, Franklin, Tim, and all the neighbors are searching for a place to rest. It isn't easy to find room at the Inn - especially when it's burned down. Sometimes, peace only comes when we stand in the cold at the edge of a manger. Walk with the neighbors as they seek shelter - and find their joy - in *The Nativity*.

Stand alone, but takes place after:
Spring Sprouts and Fall Ashes

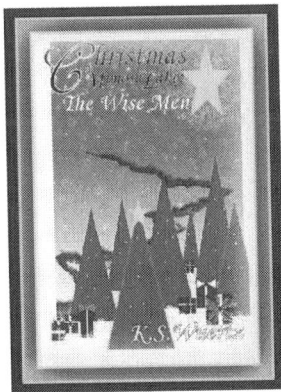

The Wise Men (Vol.2)

River's no longer lost in her own spiritual desert but she still doesn't have her bearings. Blessedly she has three wise men who know how to help her. Dock Crayton, forever the fixer, believes his Christmas surprise will fix his wife's pain. But he didn't count on falling in love while Christmas shopping. Still, the neighbors are beloved: *Good tidings of great joy* await them, if they will only follow their hearts.

Stand alone, but takes place after:
The Shadows of Comfort

Can be read with the series or as stand-alones

MORE NOVELS TO READ

SOUL SEARCHING (2015)
What Happens When We Die?

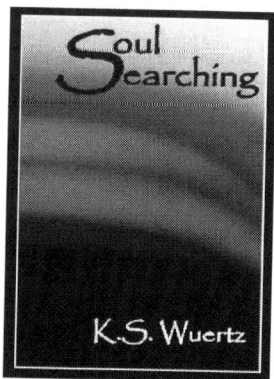

Mercedes Beecher has it all. Money. Beauty. Fame. Fortune and Family. Her life looks great – until it's brutally cut short. But Mercedes isn't ready to go. She has unfinished business. But she's not playing on her own terms any longer. And... where is she? So, her search begins.
But for what?
How many chances do we get?

DEVOTIONALS FROM MIMOSA LAKE

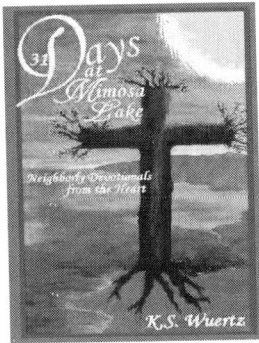

Mimosa Lake has inspired the neighbors to reflect on some of their favorite Scripture passages. Like sunlight sparkling on the water, this book is filled with HOPE! Join all your favorite Mimosa neighbors, and the author, for some down-to-earth devotion to Heaven above! The good news awaits... Rejoice!

FOR ADULTS AND CHILDREN TO READ TOGETHER

It All Happened...
At
The Old Oak Tree

At first glance, everything seems quiet at the Old Oak Tree, but take a closer look. Peek into the secret lives of some of creatures who come to: play, work, hide, jump, run, rest or just be near – the star of the forest – the place where it's all happening . . . the Old Oak Tree.

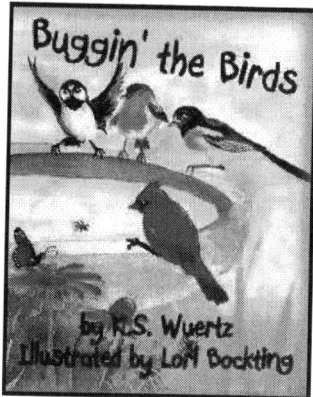

Buggin' the Birds

by R.S. Wuertz
Illustrated by Lori Bockting

What's the world look like from a bug's eye view? The bugs watch everything around them - especially the birds. Butterfly, Moth, Ladybug, Spider, the Honeybees and so many other bugs are just waiting to tell you secrets about their feathered friends.

50864502R00072

Made in the USA
Charleston, SC
10 January 2016